"Robert Smith has established himself among the best Mormon humorists writing today."

— Eric A. Eliason

"Robert Smith's clear prose and scintillating wit lay his characters bare. Which, by the way, is contrary to BYU dress standards."

— Robert Kirby

"Robert Smith has done the difficult thing— written a funny yet unbarbed Mormon comic romance, which is at once hilarious, well-crafted, and 'of good report.' *Baptists at Our Barbecue* will delight LDS (and Baptist) readers and set a new high standard for contemporary Mormon comedy."

— Richard Cracroft

"I am convinced Robert Smith is one of the brightest among the shining young stars of writers today."

— Richard Lloyd Dewey

"The kid has talent."

— Joseph Fielding McConkie

For Time & All Absurdity

For Time & All Absurdity

ROBERT FARRELL SMITH

BOOKCRAFT

Salt Lake City, Utah

Library of Congress Cataloging-in-Publication Data

Smith, Robert F., 1970-
    For time and all absurdity / Robert Farrell Smith.
        p.   cm.
    ISBN 1-57008-823-3 (pbk.)
    1. Embezzlement investigation--Fiction. 2. Divorced women--Fiction.
    3. Mormons--Fiction. I. Title.
    PS3569.M537928 F67 2002
    813'.54--dc21   2002001503

Printed in the United States of America   18961
R. R. Donnelley and Sons, Harrisonburg, VA

10   9   8   7

*To Krista, the woman who
makes the eternities seem
way too short*

1

EASY COME, EASY GO

I was fourteen when my Grandpa Smith died, leaving all his worldly possessions and wealth to my family. This was no small sum of money. My grandfather had owned and operated one of the largest meatpacking companies in the state. He used to give us whole packs of hot dogs whenever we'd go over to see him. While other kids got coins and toys from their grandpas, I got franks. My brother and sister and I used to use them as Lincoln Logs, building hot dog forts that our dog would eventually devour. You could always tell when we had just visited Grandpa because our Great Dane would be sick for the rest of the week.

But Grandpa was gone now, and his meat dynasty had been split up like a single wiener at a busy barbecue.

My much older brother, Clay, sank all his inheritance into a failing chain of second- tipping toward third-rate theme restaurants that served up movie memorabilia and really big hamburgers. Sadly, even his injection of cash couldn't make people care about the windbreaker of some unknown stagehand who was rumored to have worked as a key grip on the movie *Titanic*. "At least the food is good" was something that some other restaurant may have been able to claim—but not Clay's. The hamburgers at his place tasted like they were made out of ground chuck, as in wood. The restaurant received a thumbs down from the public and went belly-up, taking with it every penny Clay had inherited or ever saved.

Dirt-poor, Clay moved back home May 1st. Thanks to some tricky talking, however, he was able to walk away with the windbreaker and a few other nondescript items. He wore the jacket often and was quick to let people know that it was the only thing my grandfather had left him.

My sister, Kate, who was exactly one year younger than Clay, took her inheritance on a three-month cruise around the world. Four days into the cruise she became engaged to a man named Paul. Needless to say, but thrown in anyway, brains were not something Kate had in abundance. The day before she was to arrive home, the ship's captain called to tell us that this Paul fellow had left, taking what was left of Kate's money. He also told us that in a fit of post-wealth depression, Kate had used the remainder of her money to buy a couple of thousand lottery tickets, then locked herself in the bathroom, where she had scratched herself for hours. In the end she had won just over seventeen dollars. We thanked the captain for his concern, feeling that he genuinely cared, until he mentioned that in a fit of rage my sister had also broken a deck chair, and that the family now owed the cruise line two hundred dollars for repairs. My parents ended up footing the bill, and Kate moved back home on May 12th, monetarily and emotionally spent. My parents gave her a book on the evils of gambling as a welcome-home gift.

My parents.

My father, Ronald, was a great man, both figuratively and literally. He struggled with his weight as if he were Enos wrestling for a remission of his sins. He was tall and as blue-eyed as any person I had ever seen. He constantly looked as if he didn't know whether the moment called for him to smile or frown. He also enjoyed talking, and throwing out analogies that usually made little or no sense.

My mother, Judy, was just the opposite of my father, weight-wise. She was rail thin. Mom had sported the same hairdo since she was sixteen—a short bob with a flip. She thought denim was the fabric of the gods, so you hardly ever saw her without something looking as though it had been made out of a pair of Levi's. Mom insisted that she was 5' 7", although she wasn't a single centimeter over 5' 4". Even though I knew they loved each other, my parents seemed a poor match. Despite the differences in their physical makeup, I liked them much more than most kids my age cared for their parents.

Mom and Dad used Grandpa's money mostly to cover up things. I'm certain there's some hidden meaning to that. They spent it on custom-made denim toilet seat covers, toaster covers, furniture covers, and car covers. Our house looked like the aftermath of a giant denim atomic bomb. They socked away what was left over for a rainy day, or early retirement.

Then there was my share of the inheritance. My parents were determined that I spend my money wisely—and my being the youngest child and not yet of legal age gave them the green light to help me do so. I hadn't thought much about it, but I suppose if it had been left up to me, I would have spent most of the money on video games and maybe a few books. But my parents, with all their sagacity, bought a small cabin for me in my name. It was a nice place on eight acres of secluded land in the distant mountains above our city.

I loved it.

"Ian, my boy, this is a sound investment, a real security," Dad informed me. "Your money's not sitting in some bank getting stale; it's growing."

My growing investment came complete with a stove and a refrigerator that I immediately fantasized about stocking only with things I liked. My mother talked me into buying flood insurance with the remainder of my money.

"Remember Noah," she lectured, her painted lips clicking against her white teeth. "When the rains came down, he was prepared."

Two and a half weeks later my investment burned to the ground due to a lightning fire. I was left with nothing but eight acres of charred land. The morning after the fire, my father gave me six dollars and twenty-three cents, informing me that was all that was left from my inheritance. He then delivered what I've come to call his infamous "Value-of-Badly-Burned-Land" speech.

"Ian, you now have the opportunity to shape that land. Why, this is all just one big blessing. That land is yours to form and grow with. In fact, I think . . ." he said, rising on his size-thirteen feet to give greater credence to his postulation, "I think that old house would have done nothing but clutter things up." My father ended his speech with, "That house was sort of an eyesore."

Never in my life had I talked back to my dad, but I took that opportunity to do some intense *thinking* back. *Sort of an eyesore? Yeah, not like the toasted, leafless trees and blackened soil up there now. Their beauty transcends that of my quaint log house with white trimmed windows and working appliances (losing that refrigerator really hurt). Thanks, Dad, for your true understanding of the situation.*

He asked me if I understood.

"Yes," I replied.

"Good," he tossed back.

I lost the twenty-three cents and blew the six bucks on gum and colored popcorn.

2

DYSFUNCTIONAL BLISS

We had our first family home evening with Clay and Kate back home on July 5th. We sang:

> We're all together again.
> We're here! We're here!
> Here we are singing all together again, singing,
> "All together again. We're here! We're here!"

Mom pretty much carried the song.

The situation at our house had been quite tense since my brother and sister had moved back in. Clay and Kate had ceased fighting for the moment, but we all knew the intense battle over who got the biggest room was not yet over. Mom had made a total of twenty-two batches of burnt chocolate chip cookies, of which maybe only three had been nibbled on. Dad spent a lot of time in his workshop sanding things. He told me sandpaper is like the gospel—rough, and at times hard to embrace. But with it you could smooth down even the roughest of edges. I thought it was a poor analogy. I spent most of my time in my room getting used to having my brother and sister living with us again.

My father asked me to say the opening prayer for family home evening. I said a quick one with all the standard lines.

Our night of unifying bliss had begun.

"If someone would have told your mother and me a couple of months ago that both of you would be coming back home to live with us again, well, I'm not sure we would have believed it. But you're all here, and that's what counts." Dad scratched his knee and took a breath. "However, we feel, your mother and I that is, that it would be a disservice to you, Clay and Kate, if we allowed you to stay without asking you to pay a small monthly rent."

My brother and sister moaned in harmony. They had been expecting the rent announcement. It was Dad's next sentence that they were unprepared for.

"Also, your mother has asked that unlike when you lived here before, you now need to be responsible for your own laundry."

It was a incendiary statement, fired at a particularly sensitive time. Family home evening fell silent, and as sure as I knew that spin cycle followed rinse, I knew that trouble lay ahead.

Clay broke the silence. He mumbled something mildly vulgar and then stormed out of the room. I tried to pretend that I hadn't heard what he'd said. I wanted desperately for Clay to be the kind of older brother that those *New Era* stories always talked about. It took an active imagination. Clay was tall, but it was clear even now that I would one day outgrow him. He had a small nose and big cheeks that were rosy even when his life wasn't. He walked with a strut and was passionate about making Kate's life miserable. The two of them had taken sibling rivalry to a whole new level. I saw Clay reach the end of the hall and go into his room.

A door slammed.

Kate began to cry (she had become quite good at that over the previous few weeks). She sobbed about how my mother had never made them do their own wash when they used to live at home.

"It's just laundry," my mother argued. "And you're capable."

"How can you be so insensitive?" Kate wailed, her blue eyes wide and wet.

Her long blond hair was pulled up into a ponytail that whipped around as she shook her head. Kate liked me. At least that's what my mother and father kept insisting in private. I'm certain that she did, but I was just as certain that she didn't like me as much as she cared for herself. She was beautiful, and getting prettier. At least that's how her personal mission statement read. And she found her greatest joy in shopping. That and giving Clay grief. Theirs was an equal opportunity love-hate (hold the loving) relationship. Despite how she felt about Clay, it was my mother she was most upset with at the moment.

"This is just awful," Kate cried. "Our own laundry?" She then got up and ran from the room like a fugitive with only one chance for escape.

Mom kneaded both her temples. She gave the appearance of rain, but held strong, sticking her lower lip out until it almost completely engulfed her chin. She took a deep breath, flipped her hair back, and then opened the denim-covered home evening manual. Forcing a big, bright smile, Mom began the lesson, which was on family togetherness. Unfortunately, the emotional strain was too great. Her eyes were the first to give. Her nose went next. She sat there, her face a mixture of tears and wet pancake makeup, mascara, and other substances, asking me if I knew that families could be together forever.

It was too much for my dad to take. He tried to hold back his laughter, but in the end he just wasn't that strong. I, like a faithful son, followed his example. Mom didn't appreciate being laughed at, and she let it all go. She went on and on, criticizing everything from the paper boy's poor aim to the few extra pounds my father had put on. She cried, vented, shook her head, and cried some more. With each shake of her head, more and more of her hair stuck to her face and the liquid concoction on it. Her words became shorter.

"And if you . . . Why I . . ."

Her breathing became heavier.

"I—huff—don't—huff—you."

Her frustration became too great, and she ran to her room sobbing. My dad and I just stared at each other.

A few minutes later Mom was back out in the kitchen, putting together some sort of treat for family home evening. It was at that moment that I fully realized just how great my mom really is. Despite my realization, however, I turned down her offer of crackers and peanut butter—seeing how my father had promised just moments before that we'd go out for ice cream. We invited Mom, but she declined, vigorously massaging her temples while insisting that my dad and I needed some time alone together.

At the ice cream shop I talked my father into buying me

three scoops. We then ate our treats while walking around a small duck pond out in front of the store.

"Grandpa's money has sure messed things up," I licked.

"We're given a lot of things in life that we must use to help us grow."

I wondered where he had read that.

"Dad, don't you think girls are cute?"

My mouth dropped open. I had no idea what had possessed me to ask what I had just asked. It had come out of nowhere, the words just sliding out. I had meant to ask him how long Clay and Kate would be living with us. Instead, that had escaped. It was a major father-son faux pas.

"I mean, I sure like this ice cream," I said quickly, hoping he would forget my original statement and dreading the reply he would give if he hadn't. I knew that he would go into great detail about his and my mother's courtship, saying things like, "There is a time and a place for cute, Son." Or maybe he would assume that I had a crush on someone and pressure me until I told him all the sordid details. I threw my shoulders back and readied myself for the landslide of probing questions and endless sayings on virtue. But his only commentary was about the ice cream.

"I've never understood how they get something to taste so good."

He had ignored my first question and I was surprisingly . . . disappointed. I guess deep down I was hoping to tell him about my crush on Bronwyn Innaway. It wasn't a crush so much; it was more like a hope or a wish—but at this point, not even a possibility. The dark-haired girl with the light blue eyes seemed to be a painfully unrealistic dream to this love-struck fourteen-year-old. I brought the conversation back to my grandpa's money.

"What good has that money done any of us?"

A simple answer was too much to ask for.

"I'll be interested to see what you do with your property, Ian," Dad answered.

Two weeks later I got my parents to drive me up to my land, and there I planted my first two trees. One died almost immediately; but the other one made it.

3

SPIT AND POLISH

One significant detail about my fifteenth year alive—besides Bronwyn Innaway getting braces and a perm—was the fact that my brother and sister decided that living at home for the remainder of their lives was not necessarily a bad thing. It was also the year my dad's hair turned completely gray.

My father *did* up the rent, hoping it would scare them out. But not wanting to be too harsh, and having a rather strange sense of the value of money, he only upped it by $3.50 a month. After the staged reactions of upset, Clay and Kate agreed to pay the new rate.

We got a new refrigerator that year—I think the increase in rent money lured my dad into a false sense of financial security. He returned the refrigerator a week later because the ice maker was too loud.

I was able to camp for a week alone on my property that summer.

I planted another six trees and twelve bushes and mowed down the weeds. Clay picked me up at the end of the week.

He told me that they had all missed me and then kept calling me Sara, the name of his new girlfriend.

Bronwyn tried out for the pep squad that year, but she didn't make it. I felt that her being cut from the squad greatly increased my chances to make her mine.

The new school year also brought new responsibilities.

"But it's hard enough getting up on time now," I moaned, beginning to genuinely panic. I couldn't believe my dad was asking this of me. A paper route? What had I done to deserve this? I tried a different approach.

"It's dangerous out there, Dad. I could get kidnapped, or robbed, or who knows what. Just last week, our paperboy, Danny Gardiner, got his bike stolen, and they found him abandoned in a ditch, with two black eyes."

I was stretching the truth just a bit. Sure, Danny had gotten his bike stolen, but not while delivering papers. And purists might point out that he had not been found in a ditch, but he had been caught in one while spying on Laurel Yawney, and the lecture Laurel's dad gave Danny was far worse than any two black eyes could have ever been.

"Danny's a lot smaller than you," was my father's supportive reply. "Besides, you're not really scared are you?"

Desperate times call for desperate measures.

"Yes," I whined.

I don't know what it was. I wasn't scared of anything, and even though I was never the first to volunteer for hard work, I didn't mind it once I was doing it. But this whole paper route thing really had me frazzled. The thought of getting up every morning at 5:00 was about the most unappealing thing I could think of. Plus, Bronwyn lived on the route. How would she feel, me, a common paperboy, madly in love with her? What would the neighborhood think? The very idea of delivering a paper to her home each day made me blush. Our love would become a scandal, cheap and public.

"Dad . . ." I pleaded.

"There's no need to worry," he comforted. "I haven't told you the best part."

My stomach tightened with fear.

"I'll drive you around each morning. It will be a good time for us to talk about whatever you want to talk about: school, sports, life . . . girls." He winked knowingly.

I was losing. This was even worse. I could hear it now, Bronwyn's older brothers and sisters talking about my dad and me:

"Well, look at that. Brother Smith and his boy, Ian, are delivering papers. Must have fallen on hard times."

To make things worse, the whole time they were dissing us, my father would be asking me personal questions. Clearly, I was beaten.

Luckily, I was to get a reprieve. Life dealt me a favorable hand.

The first day of the paper route, it took me twenty minutes to get my dad out of bed, and that was the easy part. He got several paper cuts, slammed his hand in the car door, fell asleep at the wheel twice, and broke a customer's window.

He came into my room that afternoon for a talk.

"I've thought about it, and I think it would be best . . . well, your mother and I that is, think it would be best if you give up the paper route so you can concentrate more on your studies."

"Sounds good, Dad."

"I'm glad you understand," he said, exhaling for the first

time since he had entered my room. He walked out, slamming his hand in my door as he closed it.

I cleared my land of all the big rocks that winter and cut up and disposed of all the burned, leftover trees. Hope springs eternal.

* * * * *

In my sixteenth year, Clay went out on a limb by moving back into his own apartment. But when confronted with the real-world responsibility of having to pay extra for cable, he immediately moved back home. In total, he was gone for a whole two and a half days. Yet for months afterward, he told stories of the wild and free times he had experienced while living away from home, squeezing some pretty amazing activities into the sixty hours he had been gone—four of which he had spent washing clothes at our house.

I got my Eagle Scout award and my driver's license that year and in that order. Bronwyn waved at me once when I almost ran over her cat—kind of a nervous wave. I thought about asking her out for my first date, but it was too much to hope for. Instead, I asked Dawn Patton to go out. We went to Harry's Hamburgers where my car door jammed, and she had to come around and open it for me.

"I thought your family had nicer cars," she complained.

I had a sudden urge to be fifteen and unable to date again.

We sat in a small booth that had sticky seats and a picture hanging above it of a girl with a scarf on her head, playing a flute. A tall boy with bad posture and nice hair stepped up to our table and asked if we were ready to order. I nodded to Dawn and she began.

"I'll have the bacon burger. Umm . . . with fries, a side salad with ranch dressing and no croutons. Umm . . . and a large Coke."

A large *Coke?*

"And you, sir?" the waiter said to me.

"I'll just have a cheeseburger and fries."

"Anything to drink?"

"Just water," I said haughtily.

Our waiter turned and walked away.

Now, I'm not completely naïve, and I don't live in a box, but some things mean a lot to me: things like church, chastity, and caffeine. I probably approached the subject incorrectly, but I had to take this stand. I ran my fingers through my short brown hair, trying to think of what to do. Self-righteous bells were ringing in my head and my brown eyes were dark with concern.

"You're getting a *Coke?*" I asked Dawn.

"Yes, I'm getting a Coke."

"We're not supposed to drink caffeine," I argued.

"It's okay to drink caffeine after you're sixteen," Dawn insisted. "It helps clear your head. I read that in the *New Era.*"

The bells in my head became increasingly louder. The *New Era* said that? I refused to believe it. I read the *New Era* almost every month, and although the "Mormonads" and "Mormonisms" were the only things I really retained, I felt quite sure that an article condoning the consumption of caffeine would not easily be forgotten.

The waiter brought our drinks. There it sat: Dawn's Coke. She picked it up and took a giant swig. Then, with the force only a boisterous elephant could equal, she belched. She smiled proudly and then laughed. I sank deep into my sticky seat wondering why the *For the Strength of Youth* pamphlet didn't warn of these type of dating scenarios.

"Excuse me," Dawn exaggerated.

Swept up in the magic of the moment, some guy three booths down answered Dawn's with an equally enthusiastic belch. That did it. Dawn rose to the challenge, and the two of them began exchanging unpleasantries. I kept thinking of Bronwyn and wishing I had hit her cat. Maybe we could have mourned together; then she, instead of Dawn, would be with me now.

The manager, who hadn't seen, but had heard quite enough, came to our table and asked me to leave. He had assumed because of the volume that it was me, not Dawn, making all the noise. I left alone and waited almost twenty-five minutes in the car for Dawn to come out.

When she finally did, she came out with Mr. Three-Booths-Down. Laughing, they got into his car and sped away. The first line of my journal that night read: "My eyes have been opened. I have seen the evils of caffeine."

Clay, who had been secretly reading my journal, laughed openly about that entry for weeks.

Kate quit her job at The Gap and became a certified life-guard that summer. It was a surprise to all of us, knowing how badly chlorine can damage a person's hair. She got a job working at the community pool and fell in love with a much younger than she eighteen-year-old diver named Mikey Shepherd. He was a good-looking guy with long bleached hair and small brown eyes.

Bronwyn got her braces off, revealing a spectacular smile.

* * * * *

My father, who was an assistant vice-president of a major corporation, offered me a job with his company when I was seventeen. I didn't know exactly what he did for a living, only that he worked with Bronwyn's dad at the Brasswood Building.

We were all sitting around the dinner table, Mom at one end, Dad at the other. Kate across from Clay, and Mikey—whom my mom still referred to as "the guest"—next to me. Dad had just put a large piece of meat into his mouth when I saw the light of remembrance go on in his head. His blue eyes glowed. He tucked the gargantuan piece of meat into one of his spacious cheeks and looked straight at me.

"Ian, how would you like a job working for your dad?"

"Me?" I asked.

"You," he said, raising his voice to make it sound as if the conversation were much more exciting than it actually was. "The company is looking for someone to clean out all the sinks and drinking fountains at the Brasswood building. It pays extremely well for what it requires. Fred Oaks wanted to hire his fifteen-year-old niece. However," he winked, "I talked him out of it. He's willing to give you a try."

"That sounds like a terrific opportunity," my mother gushed.

"Wish I were in your shoes," Clay exclaimed.

"It's a big building," Kate added.

"I'd do it in a second," Mikey chimed in.

I had just pushed a fifteen-year-old girl out of the running for water fountain attendant, and my family was cheering me on like I was a blind man with one leg approaching the finish line of a marathon. I didn't want the job from my dad, and I told him so:

"Sounds great."

My father smiled a lopsided grin, thanks to the meat lodged in his cheek.

"It looks like you're the only one without a job now," Kate threw out at Clay.

"I didn't know they considered being a lifeguard at a community pool a real job," he tossed back.

"I get paid," Kate sneered.

"For standing around in a swimsuit."

"Well . . ." Kate tried to find a comeback.

"Beautifully put," Clay said snidely.

I watched Kate's face turn red with anger and prepared myself for the worst by cramming my mouth full of food and letting the taste take me away. It didn't work; I was still there. Kate stood up, ready to pounce on Clay.

"Stop this right now!" my father ordered. "Can't we just once have a nice, quiet dinner?" The piece of meat, still in his cheek, gave his voice a weird, muffled sound.

Kate slowly sank back into her seat, and for a small moment there was peace. Then seconds later when Mikey dropped his fork, Clay purposefully stepped down hard on his hand as he reached to pick it up. Mikey screamed louder than necessary, and Kate threw her right fist into Clay's face. Clay retaliated by grabbing a handful of Kate's hair, ripping out a huge hunk and dropping long, blonde strands all over the table. Mikey's earlier scream paled in comparison to Kate's. Mom began yelling, and Clay stood up to leave.

Kate wouldn't have it. She jumped from her chair onto Clay, slamming him down on the end of our long family table. Their weight caused the table to completely flip over—the opposite end clipping my father on the underside of his chin on its way up. The whole thing finally fell down on top of my two well-adjusted siblings. The sound made by all the screaming and the dishes crashing on the hardwood floor was spectacular.

Clay crawled out from under the table and ran out the back door. Kate pulled herself up and shook food out of her hair. She reached out her hand for Mikey and the two of them escaped via the front door. Mom sat there in shock, while Dad rubbed his chin and continued chewing the piece of meat he had saved in his cheek. I asked to be excused, but they didn't answer me. I finally got out the broom and cleaning supplies and began working on the mess while my dad showed my mom vacation pamphlets. I remember cleaning potato off our family picture, knowing that if Bronwyn could see me now, she would be so impressed by my unselfishness and domestic skills.

I took it as a good sign when Bronwyn parked her car next to mine the following day at school.

* * * * *

The job at my father's company turned out to be all right. The Brasswood Building was huge. It got its name from a situation surrounding the founding of Sterling, the city in which it was located. Two brothers, Darwin and Clover Sterling, had originally settled the area. They were slow boys, with long arms and short brain waves. They set up a trading post near what was now the city center and traded whisky to their relatives. Well, things ran smoothly until young third-cousin Ethel bloomed. To Darwin and Clover, the term "third cousin" was synonymous with "I've got a chance." So, they began the wooing process. Ethel was flattered, but torn, unable to choose between the two equally ungainly suitors. There was Darwin, with the striking scar across his left cheek and the ability to kick his legs over his head. Or Clover, the strong silent one, who held the record for most consecutive concussions. How could she choose? She might have remained confused forever had it not been for Darwin sending in a friend named Tim to find out from her what it would take to tip the scales in his favor. Ethel freely gave up the secrets of her heart.

"Brass would impress me," she had said, simple in all her tastes.

Well, Tim hadn't quite understood. So when he relayed the message to Darwin, he told him that Ethel liked "brasswood." Darwin then spent the rest of his days trying to make or find brasswood. He died a bitter, frustrated, and lonely old man. By default Clover, who was eighty years old by the time of Darwin's death, would have won. Except that Ethel had already been dead for ten years.

Sterling had such a proud heritage.

Now here I was working in the Brasswood Building. I felt so connected. I liked the building. I found my way around rather well. In fact, I found places that no one ever went to or even knew existed. I spent many hours hidden in those places, reading or exploring. True, my responsibilities involved much more than what my dad had originally said. Not only was I in charge of drinking fountains and sinks, I was also overseer of the two outdoor ashtrays and the executive washroom soap dispenser. My duties took almost no time to complete, and the level of difficulty was far below the capabilities of a fifteen-year-old girl, or boy. But it paid well and gave me time to read.

I built a redwood fence on my property that year. I also finally decided on the perfect spot to build my home. To celebrate my decision, I had three McDonald's cheeseburgers and one apple pie. My burnt field was beginning to take shape.

* * * * *

My eighteenth year alive, I asked a girl named Kimberly Miller to our senior prom. She was a little bit different, so I figured she would accept. She said no. I ended up going with Stephanie Black.

When I picked Stephanie up, the first thing she said was, "Your pants are too small."

What can you say to something like that? I told her she looked nice. Her mom took pictures of the two of us, commented on my pants, and we were off.

We went to the best Chinese restaurant in town. I was incredibly hungry, but ordered very little so she wouldn't think I was a pig.

"You eat a lot, don't you?" she said, putting a fresh piece of gum in her mouth.

I thought about Bronwyn. I figured that it was only fair that Stephanie be mean to me, seeing how it wasn't she who I wanted to be with. I ignored her question and put my napkin on my lap.

Stephanie was a Mormon, which was a must for my prom date. I'm not quite sure why I placed such importance on things like that, I just did. We exchanged a few words while waiting for our food; none of our conversation was comfortable, just stupid. I could tell that she wasn't having the greatest time and that she wanted this night to end as soon as possible, because she said,

"What the . . . (Let's just say she didn't say, "heck") is taking the food so long?"

I was as stunned as a deer facing forty headlights. What kind of girl says something like that? I thought about reprimanding her; instead I said, "(Let's just say I didn't say, "heck," either) . . . I don't know."

I couldn't believe it. I had just uttered a mild swearword in the presence of my prom date. Peer pressure had pushed me, and as smoothly as ice sliding off a warm tongue the word had popped out. I would have dwelt on my mistake further if it had not been for the waiter bringing us our food and giving me something else to zero in on. I shoved fried pork into my mouth, attempting to cover the bitter taste of my first and only swearword. We ate in silence. I finished mine. Stephanie, however, only had a couple bites of hers.

"Most guys take me to American restaurants because they know I hate Chinese," she explained.

I told her she had pretty eyes.

The waiter brought us our fortune cookies. Stephanie's said, "Romance is just around the corner."

"Yeah, right," she snipped, throwing her fortune to the ground. Not only did she swear, she littered.

My fortune was, "The grass isn't always greener."

At first the dance was all right. I tried not to talk much, playing the strong, silent type. The dance floor was crowded, and Bronwyn was there with some guy who didn't go to our school. I left Stephanie standing with some of her friends and went to get some punch for us. The couple hugging next to the punch bowl made me think about the relationship Bronwyn and I had and how desperately it was lacking.

I poured some blue punch into a plastic cup and looked up to see Stephanie standing next to me, holding some other guy's hand.

"Would it be all right if I finished out the night with Ben?" she asked me. "Things aren't exactly clicking between you and me."

"Sure," I said, feeling incredibly relieved.

They wanted more from me.

"Do you think we could use your car? Ben's been grounded from driving for a month, so he has no way to get me home."

For some reason I gave them my keys. The second Stephanie said yes to my invitation to the prom, I should have known that something like this would happen. She was far too pretty for me. Not that I was ugly or unattractive, she was just too pretty.

"Thanks," she said, tossing her head. "I'll bring it back to you tomorrow." And with that they were gone.

I walked home by myself, thinking about Bronwyn's prom dress, how glad I was to get away from Stephanie, and what an absolutely beautiful night it was. It wasn't my car that Stephanie now had, it was my parents'; and it wasn't me now stuck on a prom date with the wrong person, it was Bronwyn.

That summer, with the help of my father and Clay, I laid the foundation for my house, got the walls up, and put the roof on. My mom became inactive for a few weeks due to a disagreement with a sister in the ward over sewing pattern rights. Clay began writing a book, and Kate took up karate so as to be better able to push Mikey around. My father was called to the position of high councilor, Kate and Clay switched rooms, and their rent went up to $32.50.

The company my father and I worked for announced that some important and confidential company secrets had been stolen and that an investigation would ensue. That's when my dad's gray hair began to fall out.

Right after graduation, Bronwyn left for college, and as if that wasn't bad enough, she left to go to BYU. I knew I was in serious trouble.

* * * * *

Just before I turned nineteen, I met and started seeing a girl named Mary Steely. She and her brother helped me finish the walls in my house and tile the kitchen floor. She was the first person I called when I got my mission call.

"Germany," I told her.

She said she loved me. I couldn't wait to go.

A few days before I was to leave on my mission I was called into my boss's office. Fred Oaks was president of the company, and he ruled the Brasswood Building with an iron fist. Which was probably why I was so surprised by the weak handshake he gave me before I sat down. He had a big face that was spread out over a tiny head. From certain angles it actually looked as if his eyes were on the sides of his noggin instead of in the front. His mouth seemed to rest where most people's necks were. It was really uncomfortable to watch him laugh.

"Have you noticed anything unusual during the time you've been working here?" he asked me.

I said, "No," thinking about the time I had seen a lady

fall over the rail of the second floor onto six business-men standing in the lobby. Everyone had walked away unhurt. He asked me how my father was doing and if I respected him.

I said, "Fine," and, "Yes I do." I think he wanted me to answer differently.

"The fact of the matter is, Ian, there has been a serious breach of ethics here."

I could feel sweat beading on my palms as they rested on the arms of the gray, leather chair.

I spoke up, "Do you realize that there are a hundred and twenty sinks in this building?" I didn't know what else to say. Was he accusing my dad? Was he trying to say that he was guilty of something? Even if he was, which he wasn't, what did he expect me to say, "Um, yes, sir, come to think of it the other night during family prayer I opened my eyes and my dad was perspiring. I think he's your man"? This was crazy, and I told him so:

"My dad got a new car."

Fred just stared at me.

I quickly excused myself, left his office, and ran to the executive washroom. There, I splashed water on my face, try-ing to convince myself that I hadn't put my dad in a worse situation.

Clay's writing wasn't exactly bringing in the big bucks. In fact it hadn't even brought in any of the little bucks. So he was forced to take a job working at a copy store. He claimed the interaction with the common man was going to make him a better writer. His girlfriend, Sara, broke up with him over the whole deal. I guess she didn't think it would help her nonexistent acting career to be seen with a copy man.

Kate got a second job selling shoes in some pyramid scheme. She told me she liked the job because it wasn't some run-of-the-mill, minimum-wage thing like Clay's. So far she had invested over two hundred dollars and hadn't made a nickel. She and Mikey were on the outs for a couple of weeks after having a terrible fight over whether or not there is such a thing as a seedless watermelon. When Mikey turned out to be right, Kate called him a baby, so they broke up. My father told Kate that it was for the best.

Accustomed to never heeding the advice of my father, Kate apologized to Mikey, and they became engaged. Mikey started calling my parents Mom and Dad. He even suggested that we all get a family picture taken. That was Mikey, oblivious to the obvious. He was wearing his bleached blond hair really short and his shorts long. He tried to act grown-up, but in fairness to him I'm not sure he had any idea what that actually meant. He worked for a landscaping company and talked often of opening his own yard-care business someday.

Kate ran over Clay's toes while backing out of the garage. Clay then had to spend two days in the hospital for toe reconstruction. He left the hospital with a somewhat modified strut and a deep interest in a hospital volunteer named Brittany Lanceford, a tall, dark-haired girl who seemed to see more to Clay than any of us had yet spotted.

Mom came down with a bad cold and kept telling me she loved me and that she was so proud of all I was doing.

"If I die," she would say, "know that you were always such a joy to me."

As soon as she got better, she told me that people say silly things when they're delirious.

The morning of my missionary farewell I sat on the stand

27

looking at the printed program. It was my farewell, but by accident, they had printed it up on a Young Women's program cover. The cover was a picture of a young woman measuring her height in a door frame. There was a poem that read:

> I am young and growing fast.
> I am beautiful and feminine.
> I am aware of the world around me.
> I will make the right choices.

> Anonymous

Of course it was anonymous. Who would ever admit to writing that?

The rest of the program was fine, except they spelled my name with a K instead of an I. I could tell that threw Dad off. He probably thought he had been misspelling my name all these years. It was cold inside the church that day, and much to my dismay the turnout was sparse.

Kate spoke first. It wasn't so much a talk as it was a talk at Mikey. She begged him to take the discussions and recounted their personal history—all the way from the first cannonball dive she saw him do to the present. She ended her talk with, "In closing, I just want to let Mikey know how much I love him. Amen."

All Mom did when she spoke was ask over and over for forgiveness from the ward for her recent bout of inactivity. She also talked about a bad rash I had gotten as a kid and how I had ended up with a scar on my back that resembled a trombone. She then bore her testimony and sat down.

Mary Steely sang "Called to Serve." Aside from the extra

verse that she made up herself, her performance was almost flawless.

My father spoke about growth, both physical and spiritual. I had to smile as I looked at him. Despite everything going on, he had a clear view of how things really were. His socks didn't match, but his life fit. He talked about my burned-out field and what I had done with it. He also talked about the problems at his work and the importance of being trustworthy. He finished his talk, and I took the stand. As I did so, the bishop slipped me a note that read:

"We're running overtime: keep it short."

I thanked everyone for helping me grow up and then promised I would do my best. I closed and sat back down. I had never felt better.

While shaking people's hands after the meeting, I found out that Bronwyn was dating some guy named Albert Thomas pretty seriously. That night I ate two boxes of frozen fish sticks trying to forget her. It was useless: I ended up with tartar sauce on my tie and an even bigger longing for something I could now see slipping away forever—Bronwyn and me together.

Before I left for the MTC, I planted twenty more trees on my property and scraped dried-up worms off the porch of my home. I left my property with little reluctance; I was headed for planting and scraping of a different kind.

I looked forward to almost every minute of it.

4

OMISSION

My family and friends did a pretty good job keeping in touch with me while I was serving.

But there were only a few of their letters that had any life-changing effects on me. The first one I received in my seventh month. It was from Mary Steely.

Dear Elder,

We've missed you! When I say we, I mean me and Jonathan! Jonathan is a returned missionary from Brazil, and I know you would like him. He is so kind and smart (and he loves the Church and the work you're doing). Oh, Elder, were engaged! Not that I don't love you, but I just feel so right about this. I now know that I love you in a different way. Jonathan says you'll get over it if you're serving your mission faithfully. Jonathan says he knows you can make it. We went up to your property and said a prayer about our decision. (Jonathan even prayed for you on your mission.) He's always thinking of others. He's going to be a doctor someday. Right now he's working at Denny's as a waiter.

Jonathan says it's probably best that we don't write anymore: he says it would affect your work.

Good luck,

Mary Steely

My companion, Elder Kramer, and I laughed about that letter for hours. We even Xeroxed a copy and sent it to Elder Kramer's family. I got a wedding announcement a few weeks later from Mary and Jonathan. The picture inside showed them tethered in a hot air balloon, her clinging to him and him giving the thumbs-up sign. They looked perfect together, and I couldn't believe I had ever kissed her.

The second letter to shake things up was from my sister. It came near the end of my mission, in a plain white envelope with a green stamp on it. As usual Kate didn't make much sense, going on and on about her and Mikey's long engagement problems. After all her written wanderings, her P. S. hit home.

P. S. Bronwyn Innaway got married last week. She married some guy that works with Dad.

I read that last part at least forty times before I began to understand it. It was written in English, yet it looked like Mandarin Chinese. *Married,* not engaged, but *married.* It was over. All my hoping and dreaming smashed by a P. S. on my sister's letter. I had never even taken a chance. I had never even had a chance. She didn't even know me. How could she have committed herself to someone else without getting to know me? Somewhere, angels hung their heads in despair, and the cosmos shifted to compensate for this tragic mistake. An eternal course had been misdirected. For weeks I was no good. I just sat around while my companion, Elder Bennett, tried to cheer me up. At first he was kind, saying things like, "It's her loss." But after a while he got sick of my moping around. He began saying things like, "She didn't even like you, and you had no idea what she was really like, so forget about it and get on with your life."

I started to pull myself out of it, even convinced myself that there must be another for me, but then my mom called. She had some questions, important enough to justify calling me, about my upcoming school registration.

"Since I have you on the phone," she said after she had asked me about school, "I might as well fill you in on the latest news."

"Mom, I think I can wait till I get home to find out what's going on."

"Oh," she said, sounding hurt. "Well, we all miss you. I can't believe you'll be coming home so soon."

"Me neither. Tell everyone hi for me."

"I will. Oh, before I forget, Bronwyn Shakespeare insisted that I give you her best. She was here a couple of days ago and asked how you were doing, and I . . ."

She continued on while I tried to understand what I'd just heard. Finally, I interrupted her.

"Bronwyn Shakespeare?" I asked.

"Yes, Brother Innaway's daughter. Do you remember her? Of course, she's married now. She married Brian Shakespeare. You remember him."

I remembered him. Brian Shakespeare was only a couple of years older than me and already he had made more money than I would in my whole life. He worked at my father's company as an auditor. I didn't know much about him besides the fact that he was prettier than a guy should be and that he enjoyed talking down to people. He had wavy blond hair and teeth so white they looked fake. He was a few inches shorter than me, but wore shoes with thick soles to try and compensate. I had had very little interaction with him at work. There was, however, that time he had embarrassed me in front of a bunch of people by calling me "sink boy." It had made me so mad that I swiped his overcoat and threw it down the elevator utility shaft. I felt so awful about what I had done that I couldn't sleep. So, I sent him twenty dollars anonymously and slept like a baby the very same night.

Brian Shakespeare.

Ian Smith.

It was no wonder Bronwyn had fallen for him. His last name alone made him better than me. He probably never had a problem with girls. Females most likely sought him out, wanting to take on his name. Of course, when asked my last name, I never had to spell it out—a very small comfort. Not only did he get the girl but he had the name.

My mom asked me if there was anything she could send me. I asked her if she still had Bronwyn's wedding announcement.

"Yes, why?" she asked.

"I'd just like to see it, that's all. Will you send it?"

She agreed to send it, and we hung up.

She never sent it, and it took me a month to get over the fact that I was stuck with such a boring last name. I also wanted to know why Bronwyn had waited until she was safely married to ask about me.

Shakespeare. If old William himself had been a ghost that followed me around, the name couldn't have haunted me more than it did right then. I tried to be a good missionary,

33

but without Bronwyn to work toward, I found myself completely useless. Elder Bennett finally had enough and asked to be transferred. That woke me up and caused me to get my act together. In fact, I erased her from my mind and wrote the whole thing off as a test of faith. Other elders in my mission continued to tease me about getting Dear-Johned by a girl that wasn't even waiting for me. But me, I moved on. My journal read:

The truth of the matter is that Bronwyn's and my relationship ended where it began: nowhere. So, this is good-bye, my last entry with Bronwyn's name. Good-bye, Bronwyn. Hello, reality.

I did extra push-ups that night, prayed for myself, my family, and then myself again.

Then, two weeks before going home, I got this letter from my dad.

Dear Ian,

I just wanted to write you one final time. The two years you've been away have not been easy. Having Clay and Kate still living with us is a constant strain; not that we don't want to help them, but I worry about stopping them from progressing. We have felt the blessings from your serving. Clay's girlfriend, Brittany, was baptized. And Clay is beginning to come back around to church. Mom said you're all signed up for school and that you will be heading north to Taylor College after only a week back home. I'm sorry we won't have more time.

We've taken good care of your house and land. Clay's spent a lot of time up there finishing some of the things you started. Your mom went up there just a few days ago to think about some things that were bothering her. I hope you don't mind all of us taking advantage of your place; it seems to represent order and

*give peace to all of us. You have really made something out of it.
Kate and Mike have asked me a number of times if I could possibly talk you into selling the place to them. I let them know
exactly how I imagine you feel about that.*

*I know you're aware of the situation at my work, but I just
want to let you know that things here are not as easy as they were
when you left. There are a lot of accusations flying around and
it's causing disharmony both at home and at church. I look
forward to the time when this is all behind us.*

See you soon, Son. We all love you,

Dad.

The letter didn't make me emotional until I got to the end
of it where the paper was water-marked and tear-stained. I
had no idea my father felt so strongly about me. I was really
touched until I read:

*P. S. Sorry about the messy letter. I left it on the kitchen
counter, and Clay accidentally spilled soda on it.*

I tore the P. S. off and pretended things were how I had
originally thought.

My homecoming was one giant reminder of how reality
was for me. The new bishop kept calling me Craig, his son's
name, and saying that he was certain I had grown to love the
Japanese people. My whole family was there: Clay and newly
baptized Brittany, Kate and Mike—he had dropped the y in
my absence—and my father and mother.

Mike was braiding Kate's hair, and Brittany was scratch-
ing Clay's back while he was writing "go to page 14" in the
hymnbook. Mom was either asleep or praying, and Dad was
staring straight at me. I looked at him from my place on the

stand and smiled. His blue eyes looked right through me to the outdated orange fabric on the chair I was occupying. He pulled out his hanky and wiped both his tall forehead and his nose. The ward looked older. I guess that made sense. Just like at my farewell, I was left with only a few minutes to speak.

"I can't believe how two years' time can change little girls into young women."

I had heard other returned missionaries say that and get laughs. Me, I got nothing. I could feel my face turning red. I told a short story about one of my baptisms, bore my testimony in German, and sat down. No applause, no trumpets sounding, no moist eyes of family and friends looking on, but it was over.

It was time to get on with my life.

5

BLUNDERFUL

Not being a missionary took about two days to get used to. My parents tried as hard as they could to be extra kind to me. I think partly because they were beginning to realize that my life was going to be much different than the lives of Kate and Clay. I had always thought that by the time I returned from Germany my siblings would be living away from home. Instead, the situation was even crazier. Brittany's parents had disowned her when she converted to Mormonism, so she was now living with us, waiting for the time when she would be a member a full year and could marry Clay in the temple. She was actually quite a nice girl, and aside from the fact that she sometimes used my toothbrush, I was glad she was around.

Kate and Mike were still together. They had been engaged and unengaged seven times since I had left. He practically lived at our house, due to the fact that they both thought a video and some of Mom's caramel popcorn was an ideal date.

My father had continued practicing tough love by telling

Clay and Kate that they had to find their own place. They supposedly were looking.

The first chance I had, I slipped away to my land to see how it had weathered my absence. It had weathered well. It was great to be standing on my dirt again. The small trees I had planted were growing strong, and the burnt soil that at one time dominated the landscape was now covered over with green grass and yellow weeds.

Everywhere there were personal touches from each of my family members. The red flowers in the front beds squinted their eyes as they stared directly into the sun. I could tell that Kate had planted and cared for them by the small, hand-written sign stuck in the dirt that read: "Stay Out of the Flowers." The driveway was lined with big rocks, each picked and placed by Mike. There was a small wooden plaque above the front door that read: "Home, Sweet Home," with my father's initials carved into the corner of it. Mom had painted one of the bathrooms an awful shade of pink, but her effort made it appear beautiful. Throughout the house, there was meticulously finished carpentry work and final touches that testified of Clay. I felt honored that they had all taken the time to do what they had done.

I let myself remember whom I had partially created all this for. It had been my constant dream that someday I would end up here with Bronwyn. I was curious to know who would eventually walk this dirt and live in the home I had built with someone else in mind.

We went to the stake barbecue as a family. My mom sat me down beforehand to update me on all the members and how they were doing. She went into great detail, trying hard not to forget a thing about anyone.

"Wouldn't want you to appear out of touch," she said, her green eyes small and lit.

The barbecue looked to be quite a success. Everyone I had ever known was there—plus some. I had planned on leaving early, but people kept telling me how great I looked—a very persuasive statement. I decided to stay.

I was standing next to the ice cream sandwich table talking to Brother Roger Payne, who was trying to explain how spiritual promptings played into Amway, when a strong feeling came over me. I looked around, suddenly very uneasy and insecure. Nothing looked out of the ordinary, just the way things do at a stake barbecue. I shook the feeling off and tried to feign interest in what Brother Payne was saying. He was explaining the multi-level structure of the afterlife when my eyes caught a glimpse of something far more cosmic.

Bronwyn.

There she was, standing next to the giant bowl of red punch. Her right hand was resting on her right hip, her dress blowing in the breeze of the open door. Sister Bronwyn Shakespeare—the fish that had not only gotten away, but had never even swum near. My heart skipped a beat, and I was suddenly having trouble breathing. Brother Payne's impassioned narrative seemed to be coming from a long way off, and the world around me became hazy. All I could focus on was Bronwyn. Without thinking, I held my partially eaten ice cream sandwich to my fevered forehead.

I didn't know how to act. She was married, and I accepted that. Life has certain courses and rules, and I would follow. But just because she was married didn't mean that I couldn't talk to her. In fact, I found myself receiving strength from this thought. I could now freely talk to her without having to worry about saying the right thing or trying to make her like me.

I had nothing to lose.

I bravely put one foot in front of the other. Closer. Her long, dark, curly hair shone in the cultural hall lights. It created a rather glorious effect. She was alone. I decided that the best line of attack would be the simple "going for punch approach." I went for it, the punch that is.

"Excuse me," I said.

"Hi, Ian." Her lips were as red and her smile as dazzling as ever, and a whole landslide of impossible thoughts flooded my head. I decided to act as though I had just recognized her.

"Hey, how you doin', Bronwyn?"

"I'm doing good, how about you?" she asked, gazing at the residue of melted ice cream on my forehead. I wiped at it with my sleeve.

"Great."

"How was your mission?"

Again, "Great," was my answer.

She seemed genuinely friendly and totally at ease. And, as much as it killed me to know that she was married, I was enjoying being able to talk to her comfortably, as one returned missionary to a wedded woman.

"So, what have you been up to?" she asked, holding her punch with both hands.

"Not a whole lot. I'm heading up to Taylor College in a week, so I'm just sort of hanging out. How about you? Married life treating you all right?"

I couldn't believe it. I was holding my ground. What I thought in my brain was actually coming out of my mouth, just as I planned. I considered this a great accomplishment because despite the fact that she was married, she was still incredibly beautiful. She reminded me of a piece of fine art that actually looked good, not a bunch of splatters and lines or weird images, so odd that you needed to pretend like you got it. She was amazing. Every stroke, color, and shape was just perfect. And the effect she was having on me made me feel as weak in the knees as it had when she was single. I picked up my punch and took a small sip.

" I guess you haven't heard," she said casually, "that Brian and I are not together anymore. We got a divorce, actually an annulment . . ."

My feet began to tingle, and my hair stood up on end. She continued to speak, but in that one sentence she had said quite enough. I placed my hand on the table to steady myself. Divorced? Annulled? That meant that, technically, she had never been married: Which meant she was single. Which meant I shouldn't be here. I should be at least thirty feet away from her, trying to muster the courage to come up and talk to her. The small sip of punch I had taken caught in my throat, causing me to cough and gasp for air.

"Are you all right?" she asked.

"Yes," I croaked.

"In fact," she continued, "I'm heading up to Taylor as well."

I thought my mom had filled me in on all the ward and stake news. "Wouldn't want you to appear out of touch," she had said. Ha! Mom had told me about everything—from Brother Neidert's three kidney stones to Sister Wapp's improper dreams about the Young Men's president. Yet, she had left out this most vital—potentially life-changing—piece of information.

41

"You sure you're all right?" Bronwyn asked. "You look a little pale."

"I gotta go," I said. I managed a small smile—she managed a big one—and with six giant strides I was safely in the stake center bathroom.

I stared at myself in the mirror. I had had a conversation going with her, and I had blown it. She needed someone to talk to. She needed *me*. And I had run away. I splashed water on my face, willing myself to go back out there and talk to her. I needed to let her know that I could handle an adult conversation. I went into the handicap stall of the bathroom—there was more room in there than the others—and prayed for courage. Then I walked back out, hope burning in my chest.

Bronwyn was now single. Her being once married did nothing to lessen my fascination with her. I had no idea what the circumstances of the break-up were, but I could be the one to fill the void. I hated to capitalize on a bad situation, but Bronwyn was now single, and I had to accept that. As I said, life has certain courses and rules, and I would follow.

The crowd was beginning to thin, and Bronwyn was nowhere to be seen. People began stacking chairs and cleaning off tables. I felt like jumping up on the cultural hall stage and begging people to please stay and mingle. I had to find Bronwyn.

I never found her, and word was that she left following our conversation. I helped stack chairs, ate another ice cream sandwich, and went home. I couldn't believe the opportunity I had missed. But heaven and all the eyes that looked down upon me would have had to be blind to miss the smile upon my face. Bronwyn was out there.

6

THE FIXIN'S

The week before school started was the longest week I'd ever known. I bought a used car with some money I had saved from before my mission. I was beginning to feel old. I spent one full day with my father at his office. It was incredibly depressing. Although he was one of the firm's top men, those investigating the breach of security talked to him as though he were guilty and completely untrustworthy. I could tell that it embarrassed him to be questioned that way in front of me.

"They don't really suspect you, do they?" I asked.

"They suspect a lot of people." My father took off his reading glasses and rubbed his eyes with his thumb and forefinger, his balding head gleaming under the fluorescent lights. "Son, I don't want you to tell Clay and Kate, but I've put in my resignation. As of next Friday, I will be retired. Your mother and I thought it best not to inform the rest of the family yet."

This wasn't a giant shock to me; Dad was only a couple years away from retirement. Why shouldn't he resign early and avoid some of the misdirected heat he was now experiencing?

I couldn't resist asking, "Do you have any idea who did it?"

"No. The only person I know who didn't do it is me. And, if by any chance, whoever did it is still around, I would be genuinely surprised. Would you stick around if you had information that could make you millions of dollars?"

"Maybe, if I could get more."

My dad smiled and started opening his mail, indicating that our discussion about his work was over.

Every free moment I had that week, I spent thinking of Bronwyn. It made me mad that I had such a debilitating attraction to someone. Our conversation at the stake barbecue was the most extensive, grown-up—if you could call it that—interaction I had ever had with her. And it had been pathetic at best. I knew she probably needed some time to herself, but I was scared to death about moving too slowly and losing her again. I prayed constantly for some sort of guidance or sign that I should just let it be, but I always ended up feeling the same way—hopelessly longing to be with her.

A couple of single girls from the ward called me up and asked me out. I made the mistake of accepting. The first one took me miniature golfing and kept acting like it was the most original dating idea in history. I might have enjoyed it if I hadn't felt like I was cheating on Bronwyn the whole time.

The date with the second girl was painful. She kept apologizing for calling me fat when I was little. Most likely because she looked like she had found all the weight I had lost. She took me to one of those booths where you can make your own recording of yourself singing the lyrics to someone else's song. She kept telling me how trained her voice was and giving me tips on my singing. It was a dating activity I don't think I would have enjoyed even if I had been with Bronwyn.

Mom took me out to dinner one night that week. We went to a restaurant where the entire staff was dressed up as famous characters. Our entree was served by Tarzan, but Little Orphan Annie ended up bringing us our dessert. The reason for the switch was that my mother complained to the manager (Captain Hook) about Tarzan's outfit being too revealing.

We chewed on fried cheese sticks and talked.

"Are you feeling like you're ready for marriage?" Mom asked, dipping one of her cheese sticks deep into ranch dressing.

"I think I could get married tomorrow, if I found the right person." I took a bite and swallowed.

Mom motioned to the corner of her mouth, indicating that I had dressing on my lip.

Little Red Riding Hood refilled our water glasses.

"What about that Jenny girl from the ward? She's still single," Mom pointed out.

Unbelievable, I thought. Years ago Jenny Carr had made me a cake when I was sick, and my mom had never forgotten it. Of course she was still single. Her father was a logger, and she collected different types of wood. Her room looked like a lumberyard. I'd received one letter from her while serving my mission, and it was covered with pine pitch.

"She's not for me, Mom."

"Well, I'm sure you'll find someone nice up at college."

I couldn't help myself. "Bronwyn Innaway will be up at Taylor."

"Oh, you don't want to get mixed up in that," Mom shooed.

"That?" I asked.

"You know, the divorce and all."

"It wasn't a divorce, Mom, it was an annulment." I felt that needed to be added.

"Still, I would avoid the situation. Sister Crosby's daughter Martha will be up there also. And it would please both Sister Crosby and me if you would take Martha out a few times. You never know what might become of it." Mom smiled as if it were an enticing offer.

"Mom, Martha never liked me until I came home. Now for some strange reason she wants me to take her out. I don't think that's a good idea. She told me at the stake social that she's just looking for a strong priesthood holder who will agree with her plan to have twelve kids."

"Sounds to me like she has her priorities in the right place, " Mom said. "College will mature you. You'll find out that there is more to marriage than a pretty face."

"Well, then Martha would be in the running."

"Ian."

"Mom."

It angered me that my mother would try to push someone off on me and not even consider the possibility of Bronwyn.

Our main courses arrived and Mom dove right in. She continued the conversation with a piece of spinach stuck between her teeth.

46

"What do you think about the situation at your dad's work?" she asked.

"I think it's wise that he's resigning."

"He told you?" she questioned, her green eyes showing her embarrassment.

I nodded.

"I'm afraid I feel a little bit like Emma, Joseph Smith's wife. You remember the time when Joseph and Hyrum left to avoid being arrested? And Emma wrote a letter to Joseph implying that he was . . ." She looked around to make sure no one was listening, then in a soft whisper continued, " . . . implying that he was chicken. I feel like your father might appear to be running away from it, instead of facing up to it."

It wasn't very often that my mother talked about Church history, and I found it interesting that she would make this comparison.

"Of course, Mom, you realize that Joseph did go back, and he was killed."

She finished chewing what was in her mouth.

"That's right," she said. "That's why I'm not stopping your father from resigning." She wiped her whole face with her napkin and continued eating.

I was glad when the staff sang "Happy Birthday" to an elderly gentleman at the table next to us. The noise made it difficult to talk, giving me time to get a few good bites in.

"We got your school schedule in the mail today," my mother informed me.

"Thanks for getting me signed up, Mom."

"Think nothing of it," she waved.

Unfortunately, for me, I did (think nothing of it).

47

I made the mistake of going to the singles activity that week. I was hoping that Bronwyn would be there. She wasn't. About fifty other people showed up—which, according to the singles bishop, was a great crowd. We began the night by sitting at round tables and discussing the qualities we were looking for in a husband or wife. Then, for about half an hour, we played mixer games. When I envision hell, I see it as a really hot place where everyone is forced to play eternal mixer games. We all had to run around trying to find people who had served missions in different countries. Next, we had some sort of name learning game that involved our putting our hands on each other's shoulders and arms. It was sort of a more modest version of Twister. After that, we split up into two groups: single men to be taught by a single woman, and single women to be taught by a single man.

Most of the singles, however, stayed out in the hall having pillow fights with the couch cushions and slamming doors. The single woman who taught our class tried as hard as she could to tie in Lehi's dream to being an active LDS single. She had taken the time to make a large Styrofoam tree of life, which was covered with white candies and painted lawn green. I'm sure her efforts and intentions were good, but she kept touching the tree and then brushing her face. By the end of the lesson she looked like the Green Hornet. We all left class as fast as possible so we wouldn't be around when she walked past the hall mirror.

I was ready to no longer be single.

As the week drew to a close, my dad took me fishing. We went to Beaver Lake, which was a huge lake located up in the mountains, outside of the town of Longfellow. We rented a boat and were soon past the first buoy. We sped a few miles down the lake, then turned into one of the many inlets. It was a nice spot and a beautiful day. The sound of the waves lapping at the sides of the boat was hypnotic and soothing. Dad stood up to reel in what he thought might be something. He was wearing rubber wading pants, a large flannel shirt, and a pair of garden work gloves. His faded orange life jacket and a straight-from-the-store hat added the finishing touches to this portrait of an amateur fisherman.

"Ian, my boy, fishing is like the gospel. You throw your line out—missionary work—and wait for the results—faith." He scrunched his lips, leaned back, and threw out his line. He held his hand like a visor above his eyes and scanned the surrounding area.

"Not a bad life is it, Son?"

"No, not at all," I replied.

"How was dinner with Mom the other night?" Dad asked.

"Not bad." My line jerked and then settled down.

"Looks like some fish ate your bait without having to pay the price. Just like sin; maybe today you won't get caught. However, eventually you'll end up with a hook in your mouth." Dad adjusted his hat and began whistling.

The sun, high in the sky, warmed the back of our necks. I decided to make what I considered a rather bold move and asked my dad about his and my mother's relationship, hoping that in some roundabout way I would be able to bring up Bronwyn.

"So, Dad, how did you know that Mom was the right one?"

"Well, I'm glad you asked," he said.

I prayed the feeling would be mutual.

"I had been home from my mission only three days, when

this ex-companion set me up on a blind date. I had my reservations, but seeing how it had been a full two years since I had dated, I decided that this sounded like a great way to get back into the water. Get back up on that horse. Try, try again. You know what I mean," he winked as if he were saying something risqué. "It was a chance to see if I still had it in me. We went to some restaurant, I can't remember the name, but I'm sure your mom knows. It was one of those places where you had to wear a tie and jacket. Somehow during the date, I ripped the sleeve of my jacket, and your mother, bless her heart, took it home and fixed it in one afternoon. Well, when I saw what great care she had taken in stitching it up, I knew we had a future. Three dates later, we were engaged." He smiled, stuck his pole under his arm, and with both his hands yanked up his rubber pants.

He had told a fine story, but he hadn't answered my question. So again I asked, "How did you know she was the right one?"

He fiddled with the reel on his rod, shook his left foot, and replied, "That's a hard question for me to answer because I never really got any for-sure sign that she, your mother, was my eternal mate. Your mother was different. She would go on and on about how I was the one for her. Women are funny that way. They've got some sort of special gift for completely knowing things that we men can only hope to vaguely understand. But as for me getting a clear sign as to whether or not this was supposed to be, it's like Joseph Smith always said. No, wait. Maybe it was Brigham Young. Oh, well, one of them said something about receiving answers."

After an hour of no bites, I removed the tarp that we had thrown over our sack lunches. The two bags were soaking in an inch of water. I could see that our thermos had tipped over and flooded our meal.

We had been out on the lake for quite some time and hadn't caught a single fish. Our lunch was destroyed, we had no water, and the blue sky was clouding up, making rain a possibility.

"Should we pack it in?" my father asked.

I nodded and moved to the motor. It wouldn't start. Dad tried but still not so much as a sputter came out. When I looked around for the oars I found none. My dad admitted that he had forgotten to get them from the boatman. We messed with the oil and the spark plug on the engine, but it was clear that this motor was not starting anytime soon.

"Someone will be by and give us a tow," Dad said.

The whole while we had been on the lake, not a single boat had passed us or appeared anywhere in our view. We were stranded. We thought about swimming and pulling the boat to the nearest cliff, but we were too afraid we would be harder to spot and no one would ever find us. So, we pulled up our anchor and drifted until we reached a spot where we felt we would be well seen. We cast our lines again and waited for someone to rescue us.

Half an hour passed.

When Dad suggested that maybe we should try to build a fire in the boat so others could spot us, I gave him a list of reasons why that was a really impractical idea, and he eventually agreed with me.

One hour passed.

We thought we saw a speck in the distance and waved our arms until we could wave no more. The speck disappeared and again we waited.

A solid, and rather boring, one hour and forty-two minutes had passed.

With hope dwindling, our patience for one another stretched thin. I blamed him for leaving the oars behind. I then spent a full ten minutes asking him to forgive me for blaming him for leaving the oars. It was not my finest hour, or ten minutes for that matter.

I carved a second notch on the boat as our second hour of waiting passed.

My dad spent a short five minutes apologizing for forgetting the oars and a lengthy twenty minutes or so comparing our situation to that of Lehi and Nephi as they crossed the great waters.

The third hour brought with it a large dose of discouragement, sprinkled with a heavy dash of really stupid conversation.

"Dad, you know how Joseph Smith loved to play that stick pulling game?"

"Yeah. He was pretty good at it, too."

"That's my point," I said. "Do you think he was truly good at it, or do you think people just let him win because he was a prophet? I mean, if I was playing him, I'm pretty sure that I would let him win, out of respect and all."

"I never really thought of it that way," Dad said.

"I mean—" I would have gone on, but Dad spotted a boat and stood up waving. It was a giant houseboat with about thirty kids hanging off it. They yelled at us, we yelled at them, and in a matter of minutes our boat was hooked to theirs, and we were on our way back to the marina.

They served us pink punch and some sort of hard cookies that were delicious. The family's name was Benderholden, and they had an amazing number of kids on board with them. One of the children kept telling me that I looked like the guy they bought their worms from. Their houseboat moved very slowly, giving all the children time to feel extremely comfortable around us. Enough so that they could jump on us, pull my dad's hair, and break his fishing pole. I thought back fondly of our private, quiet, stranded boat and looked forward to the land ahead. Once back on dry land my dad gave them some money because they were complaining about the high price of gas.

We drove home in silence—stopping only once to put away more than our share at an all-you-can-eat restaurant just outside of town.

7

SWINGERS

I spent the day before leaving for school tying up loose ends and getting everything ready. By afternoon I was all set, except for the new toothbrush I needed to buy. I figured I'd leave my old one for Brittany. As I drove to the store, I passed Bronwyn's home. Things looked normal. Despite a decent attempt at creatively asking around, I was still none the wiser as to why Bronwyn's marriage had failed. But it had, and I wasn't even trying to feel bad over her being single again.

The grocery store was certainly no hubbub of social activity. I found a toothbrush—one that cleaned the back teeth as well as it cleaned the front—and walked to the checkout line. A familiar looking guy with a cart full of everything raced to get in front of me in line. He saw my one-item purchase but made no offer to let me go through before him. The talkative checkout clerk began unloading his bulging basket. At that point this shopper turned to look at me.

"Is that all you're getting?" he asked.

"This is it," I said, trying hard to remember where I had seen this guy before.

"You should have told me," he said sarcastically. "I would have let you go before me. You really need to be a little more aggressive. People will keep walking over you if you don't speak up for yourself." He laughed as he spoke, looked me up and down, and then turned his attention back to his groceries.

I didn't like this guy. From his perfect hair to his cart full of canned goods and toiletries he was oily. The checkout clerk gave him his total. Fancy Boy wrote out a check and handed it to him. After looking at the check, the checkout clerk said something really interesting.

"Shakespeare? That's a cool name. Are you related to that old guy?"

"Aside from the fact that I'm good with words, no," he answered as if he were bothered.

I couldn't believe it. No wonder he looked familiar. I remembered seeing him at the Brasswood Building before my mission. Brian Shakespeare. He was more tanned and his teeth weren't quite as white. He also seemed a lot shorter than I remembered. I didn't know what to do. The clerk gave him his receipt and Brian grabbed his cart and started heading out. On his way, he stopped to look at a newspaper. I still had time. I paid for my toothbrush and quickly followed him. He was out the door. I was right behind him. I had no choice. It was now or never.

"Brian?" I blurted out.

He turned around.

"Yeah?" he asked, giving me a puzzled look.

I had no idea what to say next. I mean it was definitely Brian Shakespeare and all, but what could I do about it? Sure he had once been married to Bronwyn, but now he was not.

I imagined all the reasons why the two of them might have broken it off. I liked to think that the main cause of their splitting was due to Bronwyn's finally deciding to be honest with herself and stop denying the strong feelings she had for me. In reality, however, I'm sure the truth was somewhat closer to him simply not treating her right.

"Did you want to say something?" Brian interrupted my thoughts.

"I used to work at the same place as you," I said lamely.

"That's right," he said, realization coming over him. "You cleaned the toilets."

"And the sinks," I added.

"Excuse me," he laughed cruelly. "And sinks. Does that make you feel better?"

I didn't like Brian Shakespeare.

"I'm friends with Bronwyn," I tried. "I just thought that—"

"Listen," he bit. "I don't care if you are friends with that lying piece of garbage or not. She was a mistake that even now haunts me in the form of annoying hopefuls who bother me at the grocery store."

That was me, an annoying hopeful.

"So if you don't mind, I have . . ."

He kept talking, but I stopped listening. I had heard enough. I felt lightheaded, but I had no desire to pray for strength. I was afraid that God would tell me to mind my own business. Brian had not only made fun of me, but he had called the girl I had spent my entire life obsessing over garbage. I could feel my face getting hot as my brain insisted, "Just hit him." The thoughts came out of nowhere and began to badger me into taking a swing. "He deserves it." "He's shorter than you." "Hit him!" While my brain hollered, my upbringing whispered, "Watch your temper."

My brain won.

I hit him right in the face. I think I was as surprised as he was. He stumbled back and fell on his rear. His nose was bleeding, and he put his hand up to it to try to stop it.

Brian looked at me. His left cheek was already beginning to swell. I felt pretty bad about what I had done until he opened his mouth.

"You're a stupid person," he snapped.

"Listen," I said, taking his hand and helping him to his feet. "I didn't—"

I would have gone on trying to justify my right hook to his pretty face, except his fist stopped me. He hit me hard on the chin. A small crowd of spectators had gathered around; they were now swaying. Through the fog, I could make out Brian walking off with his cart. He was fleeing the scene. I grabbed my new toothbrush and walked to my car. I felt so good—him hitting me back had erased any guilt I might have had for punching him in the first place. I was also pretty certain that I had hit him much harder than he had hit me. I was a love vigilante, avenging Bronwyn, even though she was hundreds of miles away. I started the car and checked the damage to my face in the rearview mirror. The damage looked minimal.

When I got home I tried out my new toothbrush. It worked well. I decided not to tell anyone about Brian; they probably wouldn't care anyhow. I went to the den to get out my old yearbooks, filled with a sudden urge to look up pictures of Bronwyn. Seeing them made me happy. Happy that I had hit Brian and happy that Bronwyn and I getting together was still a possibility. Things were finally falling into their proper place.

The fluorescent light overhead was flickering and threatening to go out. I put it out of its misery by turning it off myself.

"Call Bronwyn," a voice in my head whispered. "Call Bronwyn." I would have thought it to be divine guidance prompting me to phone her, but ninety-nine percent of all my thoughts involved her, so why shouldn't one of them tell me to call her? I locked the study door. With the lights off, the setting sun made the closed curtains on the windows glow, lighting the room just enough to safely move about. Then, as if I actually knew what I was doing, I picked up the phone and hid down behind the couch on our very out-of-date shag carpet. I dialed Bronwyn's number. Three rings later her mother answered.

"Hi, Sister Innaway?"

"Who is this?" she asked.

I told her who I was and then asked for Bronwyn. She informed me that her daughter was already up at school.

"Do you have her phone number?"

"Yes, I do. Is there some sort of a problem?" she questioned.

I wanted to say, "Yes, there is a problem. I miss your daughter. I don't really know her well enough, and she doesn't know me." Instead, however, I said, "I'm going to be going to school up there, and I just wanted to ask her how cold it was. I'm wondering what weight of clothes I should bring."

She acted like this was a normal question and gave me Bronwyn's number.

I hung up the phone, took a few deep breaths, walked around the couch, lay back down, and then dialed Bronwyn's number. Before the second ring, it was answered. It definitely wasn't Bronwyn; the voice was too nasally.

I asked if Bronwyn was home.

"No, she went with Margo to get some groceries." A long nasal hum.

I had no idea who Margo was, but I felt pretty confident that she wasn't a he.

"Can I take a message?" this girl asked.

I wasn't foolish enough to fall for that. Heaven knows the sort of things I'm capable of babbling. She would write down my verbal meandering, show it to Bronwyn later, and that would be that. So I said no and hung up.

I had done it. Sure, I hadn't talked directly to her, but I had called her—a major accomplishment. I laid there sprawled out on the floor, my mind a million miles away: Bronwyn and I had both gone to the grocery store on the same day. What were the odds?

I lay there until I felt an urge to drive up to my property. It was getting late, but the idea seemed right. I ate some cold, leftover spaghetti straight out of the refrigerator and then headed out. There was a full moon beginning to show itself in the sky. I watched it follow me in my rearview mirror as I drove.

My house was bathed in the silver light of a full moon, and the long grass that I had been threatening to cut swayed in a hypnotic motion. I went inside and sat down in the dark on the kitchen floor. I felt alone and wished I had a dog to keep me company. After a time, some headlights appeared in the distance and continued to move closer. I checked my watch; it was nine-thirty. There weren't too many homes out by mine and not any on the end of my road. The headlights came closer. It was only Clay.

"What are you doing out here?" I asked him as he came into the house.

He turned on a light and shrugged. "I thought maybe we could talk. Things get pretty crazy around the house sometimes."

I silently agreed.

"Besides," he went on. "I wanted to hear about you punching people at the grocery store."

"What?" I asked.

"Brian Shakespeare called me right after it happened. He said some crazy kid who used to work at the Brasswood Building had hit him in the face." Clay was smiling as he said it.

"You're friends with him?" I said accusingly.

"I met him at a gun show a couple months back. He thinks that because we share a common interest in firearms, we're best friends." Clay shooed a flying insect away from his nose. "Personally, I can't stand the guy. So am I right? Was it you that hit him?"

It took me a while to decide on my story; the fact that Brian collected guns made it hard for me to think clearly.

"How'd you know it was me?" I finally asked.

"It's no secret that you have a major crush on Bronwyn, Ian. Our family might act like they don't know, but the rest of the community sure does."

Crush was such a childish word. How could Clay refer to what Bronwyn and I had as a crush? And was he telling the truth about the whole community knowing about her and me? Had I been standing, I would have been jumping with excitement. Since I was sitting, however, I had to express my joy through some intense shifting.

"She's up at Taylor," I stated.

"I know—Brian told me," Clay said.

It made me sick to think that Brian knew even that much about her.

"I sure like Brittany," I changed the subject.

"Me, too," he nodded. "I keep wondering when she's going to wake up and realize how much better she could do."

"Now you're starting to sound like me," I smiled.

Clay laughed at me as if we were equals and I had just said something important. I liked the feeling.

"So what did actually happen between Bronwyn and Brian?" I asked casually.

"Her dad pushed the relationship," Clay explained. "They got married in a hurry and broke up just as quick. I'm sure you've already figured out that Brian can be a real jerk."

"I just can't believe Bronwyn fell for it."

"Give her credit for figuring it out. Brian can be really convincing." Clay went on. "He's one of the top auditors involved in all this mess at Dad's work. But because he's so smooth, no one wants to suspect him."

"I should have hit him harder," I halfway joked.

Clay looked at me and smiled. "I know where he lives," he said as if he had just remembered a dirty little secret.

"You do?"

Clay nodded his head and smiled. The thought of what he might have in mind exhilarated and frightened me at the same time. Was Clay thinking of something as simple as soaping Brian's car, or as malicious as breaking into Brian's house, drenching everything in gasoline, and then watching the thing burn?

Four hours later we pulled up to Brian's house with two carloads of toilet paper. For over an hour we worked, tossing and stringing toilet paper all over the property and through the huge oak trees in the front yard. It was a perfect house for such activity. When we were about halfway done a cop pulled up. Luckily, he was a friend of Clay's. He even helped us finish. Then he took a picture of me and Clay standing in front of our masterpiece. It was one of the best nights of my life. The paper the next day had a giant photo of what we had done, calling the act one of the greatest toilet papering accomplishments ever. There was a small article underneath about some environmentalists who were calling the incident the greatest intentional waste of wood since the Lumber Day Tree Massacre of '92. I was glad I didn't take toilet paper so seriously. I was also thankful for Clay. I never looked at him the same way again.

8

FOREVER BOB

I rolled down my car window. The air was cool. I stuck my arm out the window and let the wind airplane it up and down, depending on the angle of my hand. I passed other cars full of students and luggage and could only assume that they were heading the same place I was.

I wanted so desperately to feel like I was leaving something behind—good-bye, old life; hello, new. But try as I might I could not suppress my excitement enough to create a melancholy mood. Somewhere up ahead Bronwyn was waiting.

Clouds moved in and out. Then, as if they had grown bored, they pushed off, leaving only a smear of cotton in their wake. I stopped at a small gas station in the single-building town of Forget to buy a drink and gas up.

"Is that gonna do it?" the tall, thin cowboy cashier asked, eyeing my can of juice.

"I also had ten dollars on pump one," I said, pulling out my wallet.

"Wait a minute," some guy from behind me said. "I had ten dollars on pump one."

"Excuse me?" I said, turning around to find that this guy was a police officer.

The cop spoke up again, this time directing his conversation to the cashier.

"Stick, I think this kid here is trying to cheat you out of some money. You trying to pay for less gas then you got?" he asked.

"No." I looked out the window to see if I had been right about being on pump one. I was right. "I had ten dollars worth on pump one, look for yourself," I said, pointing out the window. He ignored me.

"Stick, you better check all your pumps; I got a feeling this kid's pulling our legs."

Stick looked down at his legs. He looked back up. He slid open the small window behind the counter and peered out.

"You do it," he said to Bob, as if he couldn't be bothered by the extra work it would involve.

Officer Bob shook his head and walked behind the counter. Visions of being locked up in a small jail for life flashed through my head. My innocence depended upon a plump, mustached cop named Bob, who had a half-eaten bag of pork rinds tucked in his ample waistband. I supposed he was saving the rest for later.

"It's a good thing I've filled in here before," he bragged.

I couldn't contain my joy.

Bob pushed a few buttons. "Oops, I think I wiped it all out; Stick, could you get me Sheriff Hooten on the phone," he commanded.

"This is ridiculous," I said. "Just look out the window."

"I don't need to look to know I'm right. Wait a second, here they are." Bob then read off the pumps and the pump totals. "Pump one $10.00 even." He looked me up and down with triumph. "Pump two nothing; pump three $2.12; pump four $11.59; pump five nothing."

Something clicked in his head.

"Stick, is pump four the one by the air hose?" Bob asked.

"Cut me some slack," Stick complained. "I ain't been outside for so long, I can't remember."

"Well," Bob smiled, "for the sake of argument let's just say that I was on pump four, not one. Sorry, son, I always get those two numbers mixed up."

Common mistake, I thought.

"What with the price of gas zooming up and all, you just can't be too careful." Bob thrust both his thumbs up into the air as he said *zooming*.

"That's all right," I said, mentally making a note never to fill up here again.

In the spirit of friendship, Officer Bob pulled the bag of pork rinds from his pants and offered me some. I declined, allowing him to finish off the bag all by himself. The dry rinds created a dust that sprayed liberally out of his mouth each time he chomped down. Bob set down the rinds and put the can of juice I had bought into a big paper bag and handed it to me.

"Sorry about the mess-up," he said. "You know how things get."

"Forget about it."

"Forgotten," Bob said, bowing his head slightly.

Once back in my car, I wrote down the entire incident word for word on some scrap paper. I wanted to make sure I could rewrite it accurately in my journal later. As I passed a giant billboard advertising a half-pound pig burger, it reminded me of Bob and his pork rinds. I decided to fast the rest of the day; it was a very easy thing to do.

I arrived at the school about four in the afternoon. The campus was small but pretty. The red brick buildings were shaded by lots of trees covered with fall foliage. One building—the largest—had a gray dome on top of it, painted with the words: "Taylor College."

I found my apartment with little trouble and got hold of the manager, who gave me my key and told me to call him if I had any questions. As I inserted my key into my door, I could feel someone twisting the knob from the other side. The door swung open, and there, no more than two feet away, stood a guy whom I assumed was my new roommate. Now, I don't usually like to judge people on their appearance, but this was an extreme case. This guy was tall and skinny, like Ichabod Crane. He was much too tan, and the top of his head was covered with what looked to be a thin coat of white cream. He had ankle and wrist weights on and a T-shirt that read "Bolivia's the Best" tucked into corduroy, knee-length shorts. He had a big grin on his face, and he stuck out his hand.

"Ian Smith?" he asked.

"Yes," I confirmed.

"Nice to finally meet you—I've been waiting all week. My name is Edward, but please, call me Ed. Come in, come in. You're Mormon I assume?"

I nodded.

Ed smiled, delighted by my nod. "So, did you serve?" he asked.

"Excuse me?"

"Did you serve a mission?" he clarified.

"Yes, I went to Germany," I answered.

"Hamburg?" he asked.

"No, Munich."

"Guten tag," he bowed. "How long you been back?"

"Almost two weeks now."

"I've been back almost five years," he bragged. "I served in Bolivia." He pointed to his T-shirt.

"I've lived in this apartment almost two years, and as you can see I've decorated it like my first love. Have a seat," he said, motioning to a long green couch.

I sat.

"These your bags here?" Ed asked.

I thought about being sarcastic, but I held back. "Yes."

Ed grabbed them and quickly hauled them into what was apparently my room. I only had time to think two unflattering thoughts about him before he was back and standing in front of me.

"Why don't you get acquainted with the apartment while I try and find something," Ed said, running off again.

The apartment was nice and big, and definitely decorated by an unmarried returned missionary. There was a short list taped to the refrigerator, which read:

> *MARRIAGE MUSTS*
> *1. MUST speak Spanish (and speak it well).*
> *2. MUST have dark hair (preferably long).*
> *3. MUST love children of all nationalities.*

It became quite clear to me why Ed was still single. A small plaque on the wall read "Remember Bolivia."

Ed was by my side again, holding some sort of wooden instrument.

"Would you like to hear a little music?" he asked.

He walked over to a console and opened the metal doors to reveal what appeared to be at least five thousand dollars worth of stereo equipment. He pressed power, and hundreds of lights flashed on. He pressed play, and I instantly realized that there were speakers in each corner of the room. They had been hard to spot at first, being partially hidden by large Bolivian tree leaves. Some sort of music began playing. It got louder and louder, finally leveling out at a volume just under the sound of a ticked-off elephant during mating season.

I looked at Ed, who was swaying to the music. He put his big lips to the wooden instrument he was holding and began to play. It was awful. When someone began to sing in Spanish on the tape, Ed laid his instrument down and began to sing also. It was even worse than his playing. The music was way too loud. I yelled at him, but he couldn't hear me. When I put my hands over my ears, he put his hands over his heart and continued singing. I could faintly hear banging from the apartment above. I jumped up and mashed the power button. With the stereo off, the banging on the ceiling was clearly evident.

"Hey!" Ed complained.

"It's too loud; can't you hear the people banging upstairs?"

"Oh, they do that all the time," Ed said.

He started to reach for the power button.

"Ed, haven't you ever heard of tinnitus?"

"What's that?" he asked.

He was sweating and the cream on his scalp had begun to run down into his eyes.

"I got to wash this off," he yelled, as he bolted for the bathroom.

I had my doubts about my new roommate.

I walked down the hall to check out the room that had brought us together. It was good-sized with relatively few holes and dents in the walls. I lay down to test out the bed. Apparently it was comfortable; the next thing I knew it was six the following morning. I was surprised that Ed hadn't awakened me to tuck me in Bolivian style. I had arranged to board at one of the best apartments, and now it looked like I was stuck with one of the weirdest roommates. I also was discouraged by the few coeds I had seen as I was driving into town. Bronwyn would stand out as an incredibly great catch. Any number of guys would be anxious to date her. I could feel her slipping through my fingers already.

I said a prayer while lying in bed, hoping the heavens would overlook my informality.

I wiggled my feet and hands, testing my newly awakened limbs. I could hear Ed snoring off in his room. I was glad I wasn't a light sleeper. I got up and opened my toffee-colored miniblinds and gazed out the window. A few students were out already, walking around. Everyone seemed to be sporting the exact same color of teal blue backpacks slung over their shoulders. School had begun.

I wanted to warm up some muffins in the microwave, but there was a lock on it. So I had cold muffins and a bowl of cold cereal with four spoonfuls of sugar on it.

The schedule my mom had signed me up for was a nightmare. After deciphering the numbers and codes, I realized that she had signed me up for a math class that I had specifically asked her not to give me my first semester. I was also signed up for English, a physical fitness class, and two marriage prep classes. I was furious with myself for not going over my schedule sooner. Mom had gotten all my classes on Monday, Wednesday, and Friday, but that was all that was right. I showered, dressed, and raced to the registrar's office to clear things up.

After waiting in a short line, I spoke to a boxy woman who smelled of citrus. She explained to me how things worked, doing so without taking a breath:

"You'll need to attend each of these classes and obtain a drop card from each of the teachers. Report back here with the signed cards, your old schedule, and the numbers and times of the classes you were supposed to have. Remember, not all desired classes may still be available at this late time. Any class you do not have a drop card for will remain on your record, and you will be required to attend and participate or receive an automatic failing grade. The offices will be open until seven tonight to correct problems such as this, and I suggest you bring your materials back as soon as possible, or you may find yourself locked into classes you don't want or need. Any questions?"

I thought she had made things pretty clear.

First hour was math, a class I would need to drop. Numbers and I had never spoken the same language. I jogged over, hoping to get there early and get my card signed without having to actually sit through class.

I followed the numbers until I found the room. There was no one there yet except for one girl in the front row. A girl with hair almost identical to Bronwyn's. In fact everything about her reminded me of Bronwyn. She sighed and shifted in her seat, unaware of my being there. I stood in the doorway trying to catch my unbelieving breath. It was her. Fate was already doing its job. I scooted along the back wall and like a real man took the seat right behind her. Of course I was ten rows back. I held my desktop tightly as I tried to compose myself. I was such a coward. The heavens had conspired, trying to throw us together, and I was too cowardly to walk through the open door.

Silently, I moved one desk up and one desk over.

She didn't notice.

I moved one up and one over again, still undetected. Blame it on my intense desire to have her notice me, or the extra sugar on my cereal that morning, either way I found enough nerve to move diagonally up, desk by desk, until I was sitting on the same row but ten seats over. There was still no one else in the room, and I felt pretty confident that she wasn't aware of me yet. Then she spoke.

"Having a hard time finding a good desk, Ian?" she said, not looking up from the book she was reading.

"All those other desks were too wobbly," I shook my current desk to check for wobbliness. "This one looks all right."

She looked at me with her blue eyes and shrugged. I didn't know what to do; her glance had rendered me speechless and stapled my body to the seat of my desk. I wanted to say something; I also wanted to defend my choice of the word *wobbly*: it was an ugly word. I felt she deserved an explanation.

"I . . ." I started to say, but a large guy with one of those teal blue backpacks sat down between us, blocking my view. I hung my head in defeat only to glance over and see her

71

smiling at me. The guy's big head blocked almost half her smile, but the rapture I felt from it was complete. It looked like I would be taking math this semester after all.

The teacher came in and took his place at the head of the class. He read the roll. Most of the students said things like "present," "right here," or "yep." I felt I set myself apart from the crowd by giving a simple, mature, "yes."

"No use wasting our time slowly emerging ourselves in math," the teacher droned. "Let's dive right in."

The entire class came alive with the sound of backpacks being unzipped and calculators being pulled out. Machines with more buttons on them than I could count in a day now sat on each of the other student's desk. I looked down in my palm at the small calculator I had gotten free with the purchase of two binders and a roll of scotch tape. I was in trouble. This class was way beyond me. Even with Bronwyn sitting there, I still had a tremendous impulse to dash out. I could go to the bathroom and never come back, or fake like I knew someone outside the door and run to meet them.

The teacher called my name and asked me to solve a problem he had written on the board.

"My mom signed me up," I blurted out.

The entire class laughed.

Like a fool I let myself babble on. "I was on a mission, and she had to get me registered, and I didn't know she had signed me up for math and . . ." People were actually holding their stomachs they were laughing so hard. I looked at Bronwyn. While laughing so hard she was struggling to breathe, she seemed to smile at me.

Finally, I shut up, and the teacher called on someone else,

who easily solved the problem. I spent the rest of the period doodling on my folder.

I liked my physical fitness class, which surprised me. I had hated P.E. in high school. But here it was just a bunch of guys getting together to play basketball and do an occasional push-up.

My first marriage prep class was horrible. I sat at a table with four girls and one guy. Our assignment for the first day was to just get to know one another. The very idea made everyone at my table except me break out in a nervous sweat. I tried to get a conversation going, but one of the girls did nothing but giggle self-consciously. Another took out a picture of a missionary she was waiting for and spent the whole hour staring at it. Every few minutes her eyes would moisten up and she would have to turn away. The other two girls wouldn't speak, and between the two of them, they went to the bathroom over eight times during the hour. The guy at our table did tell us all about his close brush with an engagement, describing it as one of the most harrowing and character-building experiences of his life.

There was a bright spot. Bronwyn walked by the classroom door and waved at me. I felt good about being spotted in a marriage prep class. Everywhere I went I saw Bronwyn. It was a small-school perk. The downside of that perk was that nearly every time she saw me, I was knee-deep in an awkward situation.

My English class was held in a giant room that was divided by a glass wall. I could see Bronwyn sitting in the class on the other side of the partition, and she could see me. English was my strong point. In fact, I excelled at English like few other things in life. However, five minutes into the class I found out that my mom, bless her heart, had signed me up for an introductory course, a class years behind what I already knew. I sat there as Bronwyn watched but couldn't hear my teacher asking me if I knew what a noun was. Well, I was a person in the wrong place, which was an awful thing. Bronwyn had seen me in a math class too hard for me and now an English class that was way too easy for me. I don't think I was impressing her.

My second marriage prep class was much better than my first. The only bad thing was that Bronwyn walked by again. She looked at me, then at the sign on the door, shook her head, and walked off. To be spotted once in a marriage prep class was fine, but to be seen twice sent kind of a troublesome, desperate-looking signal.

Before heading back to my apartment I stopped at the campus bookstore and bought myself a teal blue backpack. It was a weak attempt to fit in socially. In a very small way it did ease the pain.

Two weeks later I had my schedule worked out. I decided to stick with the math class, afraid of losing my one connection with Bronwyn. I got into the right English class and replaced the bad marriage prep class with a creative writing course.

I also got a tutor named Norman to help me in math, and aside from his constant chatter about *Star Trek* episodes, he was a pretty good tutor.

I had hoped that Bronwyn would be in my ward or my family home evening group, but no such luck. I was, however, a home teacher to someone who knew her; a very skimpy link, but we were joined.

I tried so hard to bump into her or find some way of

creating a situation that would cause her to have some meaningful interaction with me. I went early to every math class, just in case she should happen to arrive first again. She never did.

I met a guy who claimed to have gone out with her. He told me that she wasn't his type. When I asked him what he meant by his type he said, "Who wants someone who's been married before?" I made it a point never to talk to him again.

To make a little extra money, I got a job waiting tables at a small Mexican restaurant near the campus. It wasn't a completely awful place to work. Besides the money, it afforded me a periodic distraction from my studies and lack of a social life. There was a girl in my marriage prep class who I found myself being mildly attracted to. She was no Bronwyn, but occasionally my thoughts drifted toward taking her out. The problem with my relationship with Bronwyn—well, *one* of the problems—was that I never saw her for any great length of time. Sure, in math she sat ten seats away from me, but it took everything I had in me to simply keep up with the work in that class. So slowly, almost unnoticeably, the fates pushed thoughts of Bronwyn aside and covered the scars with the possibility of Annie. I even made up my mind to call Annie and ask her out. I called her right before work one night, but she wasn't home.

The restaurant was dead. By eight o'clock I had gotten only twenty-four pennies, which some guys left in the bottom of a water glass, and two crumpled dollar bills in tips. My self-esteem and financial security were teetering. I talked another waiter into covering the remainder of my shift and prepared to go home and call Annie again.

As I walked out of the kitchen and through the dining

room, I noticed a new couple that had been seated and who were looking intently over their menus. I looked closely at their faces as I walked past them. It was Bronwyn and some guy I didn't know. I wanted to run back into the kitchen and reclaim my shift, but instead I became distracted and bumped into a table, stumbling to my knees.

That's when she noticed me, kneeling in a glob of dropped cheese enchilada.

Her face broke out in a smile that turned my mind to mush.

"Hi, Ian," she laughed.

"I work here," I blurted out.

"Your shirt kind of gave that away."

"I don't change out of it until I get home. I mean, I'm done working, but I can't change out of it until I get home and get a different shirt to wear. I only wear this shirt when I work. I change it when I get home." I kept telling my brain to shut off my mouth, but it wouldn't listen.

Her date shut me up.

"That's fascinating about your shirt, but do you think we could get some service soon, Eee-Ann?" he asked, dragging my name out as he said it.

He seemed much too unkind to be out with Bronwyn.

"Hold on," I said, walking back to the kitchen.

Randy went out to wait on them, and I stayed in the kitchen, sponging the greasy mess off my knee and trying to regain my composure. I couldn't decide what to do next. I could go out the back door and end it quick; after all, she was on a date with another guy. And even though the guy was unworthy of her, who was I to interfere? Of course, I suppose if someone had stepped in when she was dating

Brian, maybe that relationship could have been prevented. I could get my shift back and then be able to sneak glances at her as I waited on others and cleared nearby tables. Just one more smile from her would make it all worth it. Or I could go home and call Annie and ask her out. We could have a really good time. We might even make up nicknames for each other, and then date in bliss until such time that the Spirit moved me to ask her to be mine for time and all eternity. Then I would be eternally . . . miserable.

It was Bronwyn or bust.

I tucked my shirt in, splashed water on my face, and threw myself back into the ring.

She was sitting there alone and with her menu down. She looked right at me.

"Have a nice night," I said casually.

"Why don't you sit down for a few minutes?" she offered. "John is in the bathroom, and I wouldn't mind it too terribly if he just stayed there."

"Really?" I asked, sounding far more happy than was probably appropriate.

"Oh, he's all right as long as everything goes his way."

If you can't say something nice don't say anything at all, my upbringing reminded me. So, I didn't comment on John. Instead I went with, "How are you doing in math?"

"Fine," she said, grinning, and obviously wanting to talk about something else. "You know, Ian, there's something I've been hoping to ask you."

This was it. All my righteous living was about to pay off in spades. The girl of my dreams was going to ask me out. Don't ask me how I knew, I just did.

"I was wondering," she went on, "if you know anything about someone slugging my ex-husband, Brian?"

"Well, I . . ."

"Or how his house became a toilet paper shrine?"

"You see . . ."

"Or how his car became covered with eggs?"

"Now *that* wasn't me," I said defensively. "Obviously someone else knows him as well as we do."

"So the others *were* you," she said.

I couldn't tell if she was happy about it or reprimanding me. Just then John came out of the bathroom and approached us.

"I'd better go."

Bronwyn frowned.

I got up just as John arrived. His timing saved me from having to 'fess up to my actions. Bronwyn got up as he sat down.

"I'll be right back," she informed him. She then proceeded to follow me. "Let me walk you out, I owe you that much at least."

"Owe me for what?" I asked.

"For sticking up for me."

I don't know how she had figured it out, but I was willing to take the blame. We stopped at the front door of the restaurant. I had no idea what to say to her. There were a few mixed-up thoughts in my head, but there was no way I was going to let them slip past my lips.

"You didn't have to do that, you know," she said.

"Do what?" I asked.

"Hit Brian."

"Bronwyn, I didn't set out to hit him, it's just that—"

I guess John was sick of spending time with himself. He got up, came over, and interrupted me.

"Are you coming?" he whined at Bronwyn.

She looked at him and then leaned into me, "Will you call me?" she whispered.

I sort of wobbled my head in surprised response. Would I call her? I could think of few questions more ludicrous. I would sit by the phone dialing nonstop if it meant that some distant day she would pick up and be glad to hear my voice. I blinked my unbelieving eyes and Bronwyn smiled at me—one of her knee-buckling, crinkly, blue-eyed smiles. Then she turned and walked back to her table with John. If I had been made of wax, I would have melted all over the tile floor. Being flesh and bone, however, I kept myself together and headed home.

It was all I could do to not call Bronwyn early the next morning. Ed advised me to wait a couple days so as not to appear overanxious. But at six that evening I decided that there was no reason I should appear to be anything besides what I was—anxious. I brushed my teeth and headed for the phone.

I held the receiver in my hand, took a deep breath, and pressed the first number. Six numbers later it was ringing.

"Hello?" It was she, I think.

"Bronwyn?"

"Hi, Ian, I was hoping you would call."

Hoping I would call? She was hoping I would call. I didn't know what to say, so I said something stupid.

"I just picked up the phone and dialed you." I was a fool.

She laughed. "So that's how it works."

"I can't communicate," I pointed out.

She laughed again.

"Well . . ." I paused.

"Yes?"

"I was just wondering if you would like to go see a movie

or something with me, sometime?" I expected a long pause followed by some creative excuse, but instead I got, "Sure. When?"

"Tomorrow night about six o'clock?"

"Sounds good."

"See you then," I said, hoping to wrap up the conversation before she changed her mind or I said something else dumb.

"Bye, Ian."

"Bye."

I couldn't believe it. We were on. A date. Our first date. I felt that I had done quite well for being such a conversational misfit. Approval from heaven poured from above in the form of me laughing. But forces from below pushed up through my enthusiasm to remind me that I didn't know where she lived. I had to call her back.

"Hello?"

"Hi, Bronwyn, this is Ian again. I guess I need to live where you know, so I can pick you up."

"Live where I know?" she asked.

"I mean know where you live. I need to know where you live, so I can pick you up, if we're still on that is."

She told me and then added, "Do you need anything else?"

"That's it, thanks."

"You're welcome. Bye."

"Bye," I said sadly.

I spent the rest of the night reading about Moses. I felt a true kinship to him because of his poor communication skills. It didn't make me feel any better, however. After all, God had given him Aaron to help out. Me, I had nothing but a knotted tongue and a clear understanding of just how dumb I had sounded.

9

TO SUCCEED OR NOT TO SUCCEED

I must have been under a spell when I made the date for the next day. I needed time to figure out what to say and do—I couldn't just rush into this. I didn't want to appear stiff, rigged, and planned, but I just couldn't risk not preparing exactly what I was going to say. I wrote down three full pages of witty responses and mature questions, covering everything from the weather to marriage—just in case we got that far. I transferred the pages onto three-by-five cards and stood in front of the mirror practicing.

Pathetic.

At three o'clock Ed came bouncing into the apartment. He had gotten the teacher's assistant job he wanted and was quite happy about it.

"Brother," he said, "I'm going to the library to study and maybe even socialize a bit. I think getting this job has given me a whole new outlook on life. There were over thirteen people," he held up ten fingers to demonstrate thirteen, "who applied for it, and I got it."

"That's great, Ed," I said. "You've needed a new outlook for some time."

He missed the sarcasm and began doing the dreaded, the feared, the one thing that he did that bugged me more than anything else. He stood in front of the living room mirror spraying Rogaine on his bald head while singing, "I'm Getting Married in the Morning."

"You all right here by yourself?" he asked once he was finished and sounding as if he were my mother.

"Fine, Ed."

"Good to hear, catch you later," he said. Then he dashed out the door and on to the library.

I didn't know if I could put up with him all semester.

I tried to do some homework, but it was useless. I was too wound up with anticipation for the evening that seemed days away.

Four o'clock arrived, and I decided to try on clothes to see what looked best. It was more frustrating than I had anticipated. I couldn't remember which colors matched and which didn't. It seemed that everything I tried on was some sort of holiday motif. Black pants with an orange shirt—Halloween. Red shirt with a green jacket—Christmas. Brown pants with a striped shirt—Passover. I passed that outfit over and settled on a plain white shirt and faded jeans.

I was dressed and ready and it was only five. I watched the first and second half of two different sitcoms. I didn't want to get too involved in either one.

It was only five-thirty. The phone rang.

"Hello?" I said.

"Hi, Ian," Bronwyn said. "Are we still on for tonight?"

"I sure hope so," I pleaded.

"Why don't you just pick me up down by the library. I'll be right there on the corner. Is that all right?" she asked.

"Sure," I said. "Is six still okay?"

"Perfect. Bye."

I hung up the phone and stared at the wall. If my memory served me right, she had said *perfect*. What was she expecting? Did she think and expect me to act in such a way that she would actually be impressed? The pressure was almost too great. It had taken me a full hour to decide what to wear. How perfect could a guy so uncertain be?

I took a big drink of water, paced the living room floor four times, and left. The cold air outside motivated me to zip up my light jacket all the way and made my teeth hurt. I had almost twenty minutes to kill, so I drove up to the town park and parked. I said a few prayers, asking if it would be all right for me to be just a little light-minded tonight. I got no reply. I tried to clear up what I meant by light-minded. I got a small reply. I flipped through the radio stations in hopes of finding one that would be adequate background music for the evening. I found no decent music, just a weather announcer who claimed we could get a big storm tonight or possibly nothing at all.

I pulled up to the front of the library five minutes late, and there was no sign of Bronwyn. The sun was down, leaving the landscape looking as if it were tightly covered in tinfoil.

I glanced down and noticed that the bottom of my jacket zipper was unhooked. I tugged at it, and it came undone all the way up to the neck where it got caught. I pulled and pulled on it but it wouldn't come loose. I tried to force it off over my head but the neck hole was too small. In spite of the cold, I was sweating. I checked my watch. It was nine minutes after six and still no Bronwyn. I pulled both my arms out of my jacket sleeves and tried to rip the zipper open. It wouldn't budge. I looked out at the library. The wind blew an empty plastic bag up and across the front window. I noticed an enclosed bank machine a few feet away. Inside of it I could see a pair of feet attached to a most spectacular pair of ankles. Ankles hooked to one incredible person. This person smiled, and even through the tinted glass and gray of night her white teeth gleamed. It was Bronwyn. She had obviously stepped into the small building to get out of the wind. Either that or she was planning to pay her own way tonight and needed money.

I got out of the car and as quickly as I could—trying not to appear over-anxious—and walked up and opened the bank machine door. I had been so happy to see her that I had forgotten about my jacket, which was still hanging around my neck and blowing in the wind like a cape.

"You're late," she said laughing.

"I read once how late is actually fashionable," I said walking her to the car and opening her door for her. She stepped in and sat down.

"Fashionable like your jacket?" she asked with a smile as I closed the door.

I wanted to die. I opened her door again and reached past her into the glove compartment for an old pocket knife that I kept in there.

"Excuse me," I said.

I got hold of the knife, closed her door, and walked around to the back of the car. Then as quickly as possible, I cut off my jacket. I threw open my door and tossed it into the back seat. She politely tried not to notice.

"The zipper broke, and I couldn't get it off."

"Oh," she said.

"It was a really old jacket anyway."

"Really?"

Her simple one word answers were making it hard for me.

"So what did you do today?" I asked out of conversation desperation.

She shifted herself in her seat to face me. I turned my head away afraid to look. I just knew that if I let myself realize how beautiful she truly was, then my faculties and simplest of social skills would go even deeper into hiding. She ignored my question.

"Do you remember when we saw each other at the stake barbecue?" she asked.

I didn't know if it was a trick question, so I answered honestly, "Yeah."

"Well, I don't know what it was, but you looked so good. Maybe it was all the stuff I had gone through with Brian, or the fact that you had always been so nice to me. I'm not sure, but for some reason I was so happy to see you. I couldn't believe I hadn't paid more attention to you as we were growing up. I'm sorry for that," she said, smoothing her skirt.

I tried to close my mouth, but I couldn't raise my lower jaw. I was stunned by what she was saying. I put both hands on the wheel and focused on the road. My whole body felt like it had fallen asleep and then awakened simultaneously, giving me that all over pins and needles feeling. This was too good to be true, and yet it was dangerous for her to be telling me this at the start of the date. How could I be expected to drive, walk, and talk right when the girl of my biggest and most incredibly far-fetched dreams had just told me that I looked good. She could sense my awkwardness and continued talking.

"I looked for you later on, but I couldn't find you anywhere."

"I was in the bathroom." I was a conversation wizard.

Long pause.

"Listen, Bronwyn," I picked up. "Before I say anything else stupid or make a complete fool out of myself, I just want to say a few things." I wasn't sticking to my note cards, but then they were in my ruined jacket and out of reach anyway. "Ever since I first saw you, I dreamed about us doing exactly what were doing now, dating that is. And now that I've gotten to this point, I'm not sure that I can trust myself to speak or act correctly. Not that I would do or attempt anything out of place or wrong, but I could quite possibly say some of the dumbest and most incoherent things you've ever heard. And if I do—"

"You remember the first time you saw me?" Bronwyn interrupted.

"What?"

"You really remember the first time you saw me?"

"Yeah," I said casually.

"Where was it?" she asked.

"It was at church. You had just gotten a huge drink of water and were wiping your chin with the hem of your dress."

"I was?" Bronwyn laughed.

"You were, and I remember you couldn't see me but I

86

could see you. And I could see your knees as you wiped your chin. I remember it made me so nervous that I ran into the bathroom and hid out in one of the stalls for the rest of Primary."

"You have a thing for bathrooms," she laughed.

"Alluring isn't it?"

She smiled and put her hand on mine. Our fingers mixed quite nicely.

It was rumored that a small barbecue joint about thirty miles away from our campus had the best barbecue in the world. So we tried it out firsthand and walked away believers. We then drove to the middle of a large deserted bean field and watched the stars. I spent half an hour trying to point out the north star and generally showing off my astronomical knowledge. When she finally could tell which one I was talking about, the dumb thing moved, revealing itself to be a satellite. Satellite or star, we were beneath it and content. If I hadn't known better I could have even sworn that she willingly shifted at least a full eighth of an inch closer to me.

"Bronwyn?"

"Yes," she answered.

"Oh, nothing."

"Okay," she said.

"You're supposed to push me until I tell you what I was thinking."

She sighed, indicating that she already knew what I was thinking. We drove home under shining stars and shifting satellites, listening to the weatherman explain the storm that had mysteriously passed us by. We pulled up to her apartment at ten minutes to twelve, and I walked her to her door.

"Thanks, Ian," she said gazing out at the stars and taking my left hand.

"Can I call you again?" I asked.

"Yes," she consented.

Her face was so beautiful, and she was sort of leaning toward me. I moved my face closer to hers and closed my eyes. I couldn't believe this was happening. If someone had told me a couple months back that I would be right here, right now, I never would have believed it. I leaned even closer.

"Ahhahhhaaaaa!" a girl screamed, throwing open the front door of the apartment and running into our arms. We were no longer alone.

"Jenny, what are you doing?" Bronwyn yelled.

"It's Margo's hamster," Jenny quivered. "He got out of his cage and is running loose. He crawled up my leg," she sobbed. "He crawled up my leg!"

I could see another girl inside scrambling around on her hands and knees looking for something. She had a net in one hand and a carrot in the other. She looked up at the three of us on the porch and panicked.

"Close the door—Kenneth's going to get out!" she screamed.

I was closest to the door, so I simply did as I was instructed. I grabbed the door handle and slammed the door shut. Unfortunately, I did so just as Kenneth was making a dash for the great outdoors. The sound of Kenneth in the door was one I had never heard before, and hope never to hear again. Bronwyn and Jenny both "eweuuuud!" and I could hear Margo inside screaming. I pushed the door back open to reveal a lifeless hamster and Margo now lying on the floor. Jenny scowled at me and ran to Margo's side.

"I'd better go help," Bronwyn said sadly.

I wanted to argue the fact that it was just a hamster. But it was too late. The date was over.

"I'm really sorry," I tried.

"I know," Bronwyn whispered. "I owe you," she said coyly as she slipped into her apartment.

I drove home looking forward to collecting that debt someday soon.

Unluckily for me, Ed had waited up.

"So the big question is, did you, or didn't you kiss her?" Ed probed. He had waited up for me and was now in his robe on the couch trying to get me to tell him about my night. "I can usually tell, but you, my friend, are a tough one to read. I can understand why you might like her, but are you certain that her affection for you is anything more than what a sister might have for a brother? I have played the game of love many times, Ian. And only a fool would doubt me when I prophesy about the thing called romance. But I'm going to have to say, and don't think I enjoy saying this, that you are in for a letdown. It pains me to say it, but I've made truth my creed, and so the truth I give unto you," he said spreading his hands forward as if he was actually giving me something.

My right foot had gone to sleep, and I was sitting on the green couch that Ed had affectionately named Ricardo. The thought of windy old Ed going on for the amount of time I knew he would if I let him, frightened me and my sleeping foot. Ed took a deep breath in preparation for the continuation of his discourse.

"Ed, I'm not sure that this is any of your business."

He stood up, walked to the refrigerator, and pulled out a jug of milk. He twisted off the cap, wiped the opening with a clean towel, and then poured himself a full glass. I could see him thinking about his response as he refolded the towel.

"I'm not sure exactly what you mean, but I can tell you this," he said, suddenly on the verge of tears.

I should have kept my mouth shut.

"When I served my mission in Bolivia, we saw all kinds of pain and suffering. I have held kids in my arms who were no bigger than a small loaf of bread."

His imagery was spectacular.

"Those kids never thought that I was meddling, or sticking my nose into their business. They just knew that I was there for them. That, in this big cold-as-metal world we are living in, Elder Evans was there for them. Can you imagine what that might mean to a child who is no bigger than—"

"No bigger than a small loaf of bread?" I finished for him.

"Hey, until you've walked a mile in my shoes, you have no right to talk to me or treat me this way," he sniffed, offended by my interruption. "Do you understand?"

He didn't give me a chance to answer.

"Obviously," he went on, talking slowly so that his temper wouldn't get the best of him, "you have forgotten the words of one of our most beloved prophets, President Spencer W. Kimball. It may sound prettier in Spanish, but its sting is just as biting in English. And I quote, 'When I die I want to never have judged a man unless I've walked in his shoes personally' end quote. Pretty humbling isn't it, Mr. Smith?" Ed folded his arms and smiled smugly.

"Ed, he said that when he died he wanted his life to be

like an old pair of shoes, comfortable and worn out in the service of the Lord. It was a quote about service, not judging. Of course, maybe you lost some of it in the Spanish to English translation."

Ed's face became a brilliant red, and his forehead glowed, making the small amount of hair he did have look even less. He put his dirty glass in the dishwasher without rinsing it and then stormed off to his room.

I thought about apologizing, but the silence was just too nice.

10

TOASTERS, LAND, AND TOKEN KISSES

The next morning I found myself full of energy and thoroughly cleaning everything in the apartment. I even took Ed's toaster apart and cleaned each individual piece. Of course, I couldn't get it put back together again. Not wanting to hear Ed's speech on respecting the property of others, and knowing that he would probably attempt to ground me if I was caught, I hurried down to the store to buy him a new toaster.

"Will that be all?" the checkout girl asked. I looked over my purchases. I had gotten a toaster, a bar of green soap, and a *People* magazine. Normally I didn't buy those kinds of magazines, but the cover on this week's issue, a picture of three down-and-out child movie stars, had drawn me in.

"Hi," someone from behind me said.

It was Bronwyn.

"Hi," I said, trying to conceal how happy I was to run into her. Her right shoulder was only a couple of inches away from me, and her breath smelled of chewing gum.

"Will that be all?" the checkout girl asked again.

92

"Yes, that should do it," I cackled, my voice warping twice in my five-word reply.

"Are you all right?" Bronwyn asked, laughing.

I nodded yes.

"Your total is $38.87," the cashier said in a flat voice.

"I had a really good time last night," Bronwyn said as I pulled some money out to pay for my goods. "How about you?" she seemed to tease, the red in her cheeks making me think the most glorious things. I suddenly was having a hard time counting out my money. The currency in my wallet looked foreign and confusing.

"Didn't you have a good time?" she asked, still smiling, picking up on the pause I had left hanging.

It was go time. I realized the need at this point to say something witty to her. Sure, she had caught me off guard, I mean, us just running into each other. But the way she had asked if I had had a good time was almost a dare for me to respond cleverly. My brain pulsed; I could do this; it wasn't as though I had been born just yesterday. I could come up with some remark perfectly suited for this moment. I was up on playful Mormon dating banter. I had read *Charly* three times—even if I had only cried twice. Yes, undoubtedly I had the potential to say something extremely smart and clever. Caught up in the magic of the moment, standing next to this girl who exceeded all my expectations of what beauty could possibly be, Providence inspired me to say:

"Really new toaster."

Bronwyn just stared. Out of all the beautiful words in the English language that I could have accidentally uttered, I had said, "Really new toaster." And the worst part was that I had said it with some sort of strange French accent.

A great silence ensued.

"Your change," the checkout girl said, trying as hard as she could to hold back a healthy wave of laughter. In the end, however, she just couldn't control herself. She cracked like a peanut brittle porch swing under the weight of my Uncle Tinker. To make matters worse, Bronwyn joined in.

I coolly took my change, said thank you, and walked out the door. I sauntered out extra slowly just in case Bronwyn wanted to run after me—she didn't. In fact I stood behind the "Open 24 Hours" sign for a full six minutes before she surfaced, smiling. My heart dropped and splattered like a cream donut after falling twenty stories. I had made a complete fool of myself, and Bronwyn had found it funny.

I hunted through my pockets looking for my car keys; they weren't there. They also weren't in my bag or shirt pocket or on the ground. I thought back to where I had last seen them and cringed. They had been sitting on that little check-writing shelf at the register. I did not want to walk back in there and have to ask for my keys from that girl who was probably just now finishing up laughing at me.

I heard a familiar honk. There was my car a couple feet away with Bronwyn sitting in the driver's seat. The window descended, and like a character from some child's pop-up book, Bronwyn stuck her head out, smiling.

"Can I give you a lift?" she asked.

Obviously, she had found my keys.

I wanted so badly to say, "No, it's a nice day. I think I'll just walk." But it was my car.

"Just enjoying the weather?" she said, trying to smooth things over. Or maybe she was hoping I would do something else pathetic so that she could laugh at me again.

I don't know what it was. Our first date had been incredible. In fact, if I had been the least bit big-headed, I would have said that at one point she even wanted to kiss me. And yet here I was caught hiding behind a sign, with the girl of my dreams sitting in the driver's seat of my car, honking at me. It was very clear that I was not the one in control of this relationship. I walked around the car and climbed in the passenger seat. I managed a slight smile—a sincere slight smile.

"If you're wondering why I appeared to be hiding behind that sign," I explained, "well, I was just spending some time alone with my really new toaster."

I had finally said the right thing; we both laughed. We said nothing on the way home, but it was a good silence. I felt comfortable and in control of myself. Like my field after the fire and the fence had been built. Things seemed secure and the worst behind me. Bronwyn did sigh a couple of times almost contentedly—life was good.

She stopped at her apartment and I got out to take the wheel.

"Thanks for the ride," I said.

"You're welcome," she said, standing on the curb, her red lips still curving upward.

"Can I still call you?"

She nodded. I closed the car door, and she motioned for me to roll the window down. I followed her command. With my window lowered, she said, "I hate to say this for fear of what you might read into it," she smiled, "but I just might like you."

The wind swooped her hair into her face and with a turn she was gone. I must have sat there five minutes before I could find enough strength to push on the gas pedal and drive myself home.

The next week we spent every evening together. We also spent the days, and almost every other minute together for that matter. We did the standards: bowling, skating, a football game, and the movies. Sunday night I asked her if she would like to come with me to my home in the mountains, and she willingly consented. So we made plans to skip school on Monday and spend that day at my home.

I was more nervous about this than our first date. What if she didn't like it? What if she thought the home I had built was ugly? Or what if she said things like: "Who could ever live in the country? Aren't there mice here?"

But for our relationship to move forward, I had to show her this part of me and hope that she would not only like it but that she would love it.

"Tell me what you think it will look like," I asked Bronwyn as we drove. I wanted to know what she expected so that I could correct any misconceptions before we arrived.

"Well," she said. "I like to imagine the worst, that way I'm always surprised at how nice things are when I see or experience them."

"So tell me what you think my place will look like, worst case scenario."

"Let's see. I know that at one time everything was burnt, so I imagine nothing but black—black soil, black trees, and a burnt-out shell of a home that once was. I know you built a new house there, but I'm sure you didn't clear away the old one. So the new house looks junky and old thanks to all the debris. And since I've never seen you build anything, I don't know that you're any good. So most likely the fence you made leans this way and that, and the house is caving in at some parts and overbuilt at others. And you probably laid a really poor foundation so the whole place is lopsided and leaning. The few new trees you did plant I'm sure are dead and wilted, adding to the overall feeling of decay and gloom."

"I can hardly wait to get there," I joked.

"Me, either," Bronwyn said. "I hope I'm not disappointed."

I reached across her knees and into the glove compartment for a new CD. As I pulled the CD out, a piece of paper fell onto the floor. Bronwyn grabbed it before I could see what it was.

"What is it?" I asked.

"Wouldn't you like to know," she teased, holding the paper against her chest so I couldn't see it. "Who's Bob?" she asked.

"Who?"

"Bob. You wrote, 'Remember Bob.'"

"Oh," I said, doing just that. "When I was coming up to school I stopped for gas in Forget and sort of had a run-in with the cashier and a funny cop named Bob. I wrote his name down because I wanted to write about him later. He was sort of interesting."

"Do you write down everything that happens to you?"

"Not everything. But I've got two boxes filled with old journals."

"That's pretty impressive. I've got one journal a fourth filled, and that covers my entire life so far."

"Quality not quantity?"

"Something like that," she sighed. "Brian used to keep a

journal. Sometimes he would leave it out and open to some criticism of me. I guess he was hoping I would read it and change. I really messed up with him."

I wanted to tell her that I agreed, but I restrained myself. I also wanted to tell her that every other page of each of my journals was filled with words and hopes about her. It didn't feel like the right time, however. I think sharing journals is a 25th or 26th date activity. Apparently, Bronwyn was much more progressive than me, and she wanted to speed this relationship along.

"So, do your journals say anything about me?" she asked.

"Are you kidding? My journals say very few things that aren't about you."

"Are they good things or bad things?" she asked.

"All good. Except for that time you helped your brother lock me in the church library."

"But I thought you liked libraries," she laughed.

"Real funny. I almost scared Sister Frost to death when she came in to return some chalk. Plus, anything that came up missing over the next five years, they blamed on me."

"Sorry," Bronwyn said. She then shifted in her seat and leaned back as if preparing to sleep. She breathed softly for a few moments and then seemed to drift off. I kept waiting for her to snore or drool or do something that I could make fun of her for later. But she was perfect even in sleep. I noticed that her lips moved in and out slightly as she breathed. Her eyelashes were long, and her nose and cheeks and chin were faultless. I drifted into oncoming traffic three times while watching her sleep.

I woke her up about ten miles from my property. She primped and smoothed herself in the visor mirror as I told her about all the exciting things she had missed while she was sleeping.

We turned off on my road. I was nervous. We made the small bend and bumped along the driveway, stopping in front of the house. She oohed and ahhed as I burst with pride.

"It's just as I imagined it," she raved.

"You mean lopsided and leaning?"

"No, I mean it looks just like you."

We walked around the property and then I took her on a tour of the house. She inspected all my work and commented freely on how impressed she was. We stopped in the kitchen, and I showed her the sink's faucet and drew her a glass of water.

We had seen each other for over a week now and even though occasions had occurred where a kiss would have been appropriate, her lips had not yet touched mine. I spread out the food we had brought while she drank her water.

"Do you want a whole sandwich or just a half?" I asked. She didn't answer; she just stood there staring at me.

"What?" I said, wiping my face as if she had been staring at something on it. "What?" I asked again. She lifted her chin up and smiled.

I think I was beginning to read her correctly.

"It's a beautiful place, Ian."

"Thanks," I said, holding my breath.

"I'm glad we came up here."

"Me, too," I added suavely.

The air was becoming very thin, and the room started revolving.

Could it be?

She leaned into me. The wind outside picked up and howled in upheaval.

Was I imagining?

Reality became very skewed. I think what I thought, she thought, but strangely I didn't think so. I felt what she felt, but feelings feel funny when intensified to a point such as this. I either needed some fresh air or to kiss her. The fresh air could wait—in fact, I would have settled for an eternity full of stale air if it meant I could kiss her. I took her hand and pulled her close, surprised that I had any command of my motor skills at all. My life flashed before my eyes as I recounted every time I had wished for what was about to happen to happen. And then for one amazing moment we kissed. I stepped back, dizzy from the effect of it. I looked over at her in wonderment, unable to catch my breath.

She was sitting down eating a sandwich.

"Did we bring anything to drink besides water?" she asked.

That was it? It was over? From my lips to a turkey sandwich she had moved, and I couldn't tell now which one she enjoyed more. I sat down despondently. She looked at me and smiled shyly.

"If I let you know how much I enjoyed that . . ." Bronwyn intimated, offering me some of her sandwich.

I sat down next to her and put my arm around her. She gave me a bite of her sandwich, and I gave her a drink of my water. I had introduced her to Camelot and she had found it a place fit to inhabit. I had shown her my soul, and she had refrained from laughing.

After spending a few hours at the cabin we drove back to

Sterling. I dropped Bronwyn off at her parents' home and promised that I would be there to pick her up the next morning at nine o'clock. Then I went to my parents' house and answered questions about Bronwyn until late into the night. In the end my dad was convinced that she was the girl for me. My mom, however, couldn't get over the fact that Bronwyn had been married and kept trying to encourage me to keep my eyes open to other possibilities. I was furious with my mother as I fell asleep that night, and I was mildly bothered by her when I woke up the next morning and remembered what she had said.

My family and I sat down to an early breakfast before I had to leave to go back to school. Clay had made the breakfast, Kate had set the table, and Brittany had squeezed fresh orange juice. Mike had come over and fried up bacon, and Mom fussed around with the chairs and then for some reason placed me at the head of the table.

"Why am I sitting here?" I asked. My whole family stared up at me in silence. "What?" I asked defensively.

"Son, we have some things to talk to you about, and we just want you to feel comfortable when we discuss them," my mom said.

What was this? I already knew about the birds and the bees. And if there were other mysteries in life, I certainly didn't want to find out about them over breakfast with my entire family there to listen in.

Everyone sat down and my dad offered a short prayer. He then pulled at least twelve strips of bacon off the bacon platter, covered them in gravy, and then piled some eggs on top of that. I poured myself a glass of juice and waited for the worst.

My mom elbowed my father as he was finishing his first bite. He set his fork down and wiped his mouth.

"Son, no use beating around the bush, so I'll just come right out with it." He cleared his voice. "It wouldn't do any good to drag this out any longer than necessary, so I'll get right to the heart of it."

I wished he would.

"As you know, I'm under investigation at work," my father said somberly. "And, well, they have put locks on most of our savings and assets until they find out what's been going on. We have a lawyer who we think will be able to set things right, but with his expenses and our limited funds right now we have asked everyone to make some sort of sacrifice. Your brother and sister are putting in most of their earnings, and we are all cutting back on some of the extras we've grown accustomed to."

What was he asking me to sacrifice? I did have some baseball cards and a few savings bonds. I could give him those. But my net worth at the moment wasn't necessarily that great. I didn't own anything of value except for my . . . except for my land. I didn't want to think about it. I didn't want to list all the reasons why I deserved that land in my mind or argue it out with my family. It was all that I had and everything to me, but this was my father and my family. I don't know how I said it, but I did.

"If you need it, we can sell it," I offered calmly.

"Are you sure it's all right?" he asked, surprised by my quick reaction.

"I'm not sure of anything, but if it needs to be done then I'm willing. Heck," I said trying to lighten the mood, "I never really liked that land anyhow."

"Land?" my father asked.

"And the house," I added, feeling miserable.

My dad gazed at me dumbfounded while my siblings stared on stupified.

"I don't want your land, Ian," he said slowly. "I would never ask you to give that up. We were just wondering if you would be willing to sell your car."

"My car?" I said enthusiastically

"You would give up your land?" Clay said, shaking his head.

I tried to laugh it off and make it seem as if I had been joking when I had said it. We then laughed and ate bacon and eggs as a family until it was time for me to go.

The ride back to school went quickly. Clay came along so that he could drive the car back to be sold. He called me an idiot twice for offering to give up my land.

It didn't bother me in the least.

II

MISUNDERSTOOD

I tapped my pencil and scratched my arm though no itch had sought attention. I had a giant math test tomorrow, and I still hadn't mastered the principle we were working on. I slammed my book shut and decided to join Ed and our family home evening group in the living room. They were playing some board game about dating, and even that sounded better than doing math homework right now.

Bronwyn was supposed to be with me now, helping me study, but something had come up, and at the last minute she had canceled. I looked forward to getting a thorough explanation from her later.

"Are you going to play, Ian?" one of my home evening sisters asked as I walked out into the living room.

"I guess so." I was disappointed that my night had come to this.

"You can be white," Ed chirped, handing me my playing piece.

It seemed that I was always the person to end up with the white pawn. It never failed, every time someone broke out a board game, I would get stuck with the most nondescript piece. Mindy, the girl who had been elected our home evening group forewoman, rolled the dice and then moved her player—which was blue—three spaces. She picked a card and read the question:

If you were stood up by someone you had been dating, what would you do?

"Oh, I'd dump him," Mindy said.

"Not me," Ed jumped in. "I would find out why she stood me up then see if we couldn't work out some sort of reconciliation."

"Gag," Carol yelped. "If you're stood up, you're stood up. You guys try to give excuses, but they're all pathetic, and we can see right through them. You should just be man enough to tell a girl to her face that you don't want to see her anymore."

"I agree with Carol," Mindy said. "If someone stands you up, it usually means it's over, or close to being over."

"What if they accidentally stand you up, or have a legitimate excuse?" I blurted out.

This was a subject that was close to my heart; after all, I had just been stood up in a way.

"You can't be accidentally stood up," Carol declared. "When someone doesn't like you anymore they simply make arrangements to meet you and then don't show up. It's a sign, a signal, a beacon saying boldly that they are too chicken to tell you that they can't stand you any longer. And that the only thing you have to look forward to in that relationship is maybe a forced hello in the school halls as you pass each other."

"Sisters, sisters, we men aren't all like that," Ed said defensively.

"As forewoman I motion that we move on to the next question." Mindy handed the dice to me.

I rolled and landed on another pick-a-card space. Mine read:

What do you do if the person you are dating doesn't realize that it is over?

I shrugged my shoulders, feigning ignorance.

"Some guys can't take a hint," Mindy said loudly. "You do all kinds of things to show them that you're not interested anymore, and they still act like everything is okay. You can't get rid of them unless you move or something."

"Ditto," Carol said.

"What kind of hints do you give that guys don't understand?" I asked.

"You know," Mindy said authoritatively. "You're busy when the guy calls, you tell him you want to do things with your friends instead of him, maybe stand him up a few times. You know, normal things."

Kristen, the third and only other girl in our home evening group, spoke up for the first time.

"Where's your girlfriend tonight, Ian?"

All eyes turned on me.

"She had something to do."

"What?" Ed asked intrusively.

"I don't know, she just said she had something else to do."

"I'm so sorry," Mindy said.

"Don't be sorry," I said defensively. "We're doing great, she just had something she needed to do tonight, that's all."

"You just keep on believing that," Carol said, sounding sympathetic.

Mindy laughed at Carol, Kristen joined Mindy, and Ed followed suit. I went to my room and studied for my math test until two in the morning.

The test was at 6:00 A.M., but knowing Bronwyn would be there made getting up early easy. We were taking the test at the testing center, so we had arranged to meet right before to wish one another good luck. I waited until 6:15, but she didn't show. I found an empty desk and started the test. The desks all had walls on them so you couldn't cheat, and which made it impossible for me to search the room for Bronwyn. It took me forever to finish. I kept thinking about Bronwyn and that stupid board game I had played the night before. When I completed my test I had to sign out of the testing center to prove I was there. The sheet for our class was full, indicating that I was one of the last to finish. I saw Bronwyn's name at about the middle of the list. She had come and gone without me.

I ran home to see if she had called. She hadn't. I picked up the phone and called her.

"Is Bronwyn there?"

"Yes, Ian, just a minute," her roommate whined.

What did she mean by "Yes, Ian"? How did she know it was me? Had they all just been talking about me? Maybe even poking fun? Had I become a disposable item?

"Hi, Ian," Bronwyn said. "Can you hold on?"

"Sure," I said reluctantly. Was this one of her hints or tactics? Was I reading the situation wrong?

"I'm back," she said. "Are you still there?"

Did she think I would give up that easy?

"I'm still here."

"How do you think you did on the math test?" she asked.

"Okay, I guess. I waited for you until almost fifteen after. Were you late, or did you get there earlier?"

"I was half an hour late and I had forgotten my ID. I guess I stayed up too late last night."

"Studying?"

"No, I was just talking with my roommates until really late."

The hints were there, all the warning signs that Carol had talked about. I didn't know what to do; according to the board game I was in trouble. And according to Mindy, Carol, and Kristen I should get a clue and pack it in.

"Oh, that sounds bad," Bronwyn said. "Here I stood you up and then make it sound like I was just goofing around with my roommates."

"No, it's all right," I said with low enthusiasm.

"It's not all right; my roommate Lindie got dumped last night. And everyone else had to go out, but I just couldn't leave her alone. I wanted to tell you, but when I talked to you she was in the room, and I didn't know if she would want me to be telling people. Do you forgive me?" Bronwyn asked.

"There's nothing to forgive you for. I haven't thought about it since."

"Yes you have. Can I make it up to you tonight?" she asked.

"You can try."

"I'll tell you what," she said. "I'm going to take you out tonight."

"I think I can clear some space on my calendar. What time and where?"

"Four o'clock at the Lamoni building."

"I'll be there."

"So will I," she said with feeling.

I hung up, pulled out the dating board game, and read every question—I was going to be prepared for tonight. Then I took a shower and hurried to the rendezvous spot and waited.

And waited.

And waited.

"What time is it now?" I asked the girl at the building's reception desk.

"Four fifty-one," she whined.

"Can I use this phone?" I asked, pointing to the one on her desk.

"I guess so, but make it quick."

I dialed Bronwyn's number and talked to Lindie.

"She's not here, Ian. Let me see if Margo knows where she is."

There was a long pause as Lindie talked to Margo.

"Margo said Bronwyn went out with some friends. She left about and hour ago. Went to go see a movie or something. At least that's what Margo says."

I was speechless—so speechless that Lindie eventually hung up on me. It all made perfect sense now. Bronwyn really did want it over with. I was sick in the stomach. She was sending me signals, and I had finally unscrambled them to decipher the awful truth. How could it be?

It was ending.

That dumb game had been right. I was devastated, mad, confused, and being a guy, I reacted to it the only way I knew how. I turned my cold heart to the possibility of revenge. I ran home and got my little black book—which was actually brown—and called one of the many numbers—okay, one of three.

"Hi, is Annie there?"

The girl on the other end of the line had to think about it a minute.

"Annie who?" she finally said.

"I don't know her last name. She's got blonde hair and seems to be somewhat mild tempered." I was in a really bad mood. "I'm in her marriage prep class. That Annie. That's the one I want to talk to. Would that be all right with you, or should I call back later when you're not home?" I tried to sound irritated in the nicest way.

I began to hear faint sniffling and then sobs.

"For your information, there is no one named Annie living here," she finally said, taking a giant breath of air. "Plus I just burnt my TV dinner. I got all of my money stolen yesterday, and I share a room with a girl who snores and is antisocial to the point of being a recluse. My other two roommates are mean, and I wish I had never left home to come to this horrible place where guys with better-than-thou attitudes like you run rampant."

I had really done it. It was completely opposite to my nature to be mean to people, especially girls. But I was so upset over what was happening that I wasn't acting like myself at all. I said a silent prayer, begging to be able to calm this hysterical girl and pleading to please have this lesson in humility be postponed until a more convenient time. I thought seriously about hanging up. After all, I hadn't given my name yet.

"Look," I sighed. "I obviously dialed the wrong number. I'm sorry that I said all that. I had no right. I guess I'm just in a rotten mood. I don't even know you and I'm biting your head off. I've just had a really dumb day. I shouldn't have taken it out on you."

She sort of sighed and then caught her breath.

"It's all right," she sniffled. "I should have been nicer, too."

All I had to say was good-bye, and maybe thanks, but I blew it.

My mouth started throwing out unauthorized words. "I know we don't know one another, and I definitely made a bad first impression. But would you like to go see a movie or something tonight?" I suppose I still needed something to cover the hurt of Bronwyn.

"It's kind of late notice, . . . but if the movie's good enough, sure."

What was I doing?

"I'll pick you up about eight if that's all right."

"Sure," she said, warming up to the idea. "I'm in the Pioneer Apartments, number 4-G."

"I'll see you at eight," I said, sealing my fate.

I had reached to hang up the phone when I heard what sounded like a desperate scream coming out of the receiver.

I put it back to my ear. "What's wrong?" I asked.

"I don't even know your name."

It was a reasonable request. "Oh, right. I'm Ian."

"Even? What kind of a name is that?"

"No. Ian."

"Spell it."

"I–A–N. You know, Ian. What's yours?"

"I'm Sharon. Did you say eight?"

"Right."

We hung up.

What had I done? I was in for it. I was going to see an unknown movie with a wrong number. A blind date. A date that I had set up. I had no one to blame but myself, and maybe Bronwyn. Oh, she would get a kick out of this; her standing me up was a huge gash, and me spending the night on some hideous blind date was lemon flavored salt poured into that wound. I didn't even know how old this girl was or what she was like. If I had had a reputation to uphold, I would have been pretty worried.

Ed came into the kitchen and got a glass out of the cupboard.

"Hey, Ed, what are you doing tonight?"

He held the glass up to the kitchen light looking for spots.

"Oh, bother," he said.

He had found a spot. He went to the kitchen cabinets and took out a roll of unopened paper towels. He used a small pen knife to slit the seam of the package and then carefully opened it up. He took the paper towels out, folded the plastic wrap, and disposed of it. He put the paper towels into the paper towel holder and took the first sheet off.

"It just so happens," he finally answered, "that I'm not doing a thing tonight. Why, do you want to go see a movie or something?" he asked.

"No," I said a little too quickly. "Actually, I made the mistake of asking some girl that I don't even know out on a date. And I was wondering if maybe you might want to take her out instead of me?"

"You asked out someone besides Bronwyn?"

"It's a long story and a big mistake."

He polished the spot off the glass, then proceeded to pour

himself a full glass of grapefruit juice. He lifted the juice to his mouth, and with three strong gulps and some intense Adam's apple movement, he downed the whole helping. He set the glass down on the counter and breathed in.

"Does she speak Spanish?" He asked.

"What?"

"Does this girl you want me to take out speak Spanish?"

"I don't know, Ed."

"Convert or lifer?" he asked.

"Come on, Ed, I have no idea. Will you take her out or not?"

He fidgeted with his belt a little, then held his cheeks between his hands as he considered the proposition.

"I'll do it," he finally said.

"You will?" My heart jumped for joy. I had gotten myself out of a character building experience with only a small amount of effort or character building. I felt a tinge of pain for this poor girl who had just become Ed's date, but it was fleeting.

"Of course . . ." Ed said.

Of course what? I thought.

"I'm not sure I want to do this all alone, so maybe it would be best if you came along with us," Ed said, smiling.

"Oh, you don't want me there," I said quickly. "I'd be nothing but a third wheel."

"Don't put yourself down," Ed insisted. "We'd love to have you around."

"Ed."

"I'm not doing this alone," he insisted. "You only have to sit there. I'll do all the wooing."

"I've sort of made it a personal goal to be at least two miles away when you're actually doing any wooing."

"You might learn a thing or two," Ed sniffed.

"Come on, Ed," I begged.

"All right," he bartered. "You come with us for the first few minutes. If things are going well, and you can think up a believable excuse to slip away, then I'll let you."

My guardian angel was pathetic at steering me away from danger.

"All right," I consented. Oddly enough, being with Ed and this girl seemed better than being alone with only her. "You'd better hurry and get ready, we have to be there by eight."

Ed whooped, jumping up and running to the bathroom. He slammed the door shut and began singing while running water. It suddenly occurred to me that I had never seen Ed out with a girl. He talked all the time about a girl named Amanda, whom he had left at home brokenhearted and on the brink of joining a convent due to the fact that she couldn't have his love. But I had never actually seen him out on a date. This was going to be some evening.

I thought about Bronwyn. She had done this to me. She had tired of me, and like Carol said, she was now too chicken to actually tell me. I had thought things were great. I must just be one of those dumb guys that doesn't know up from down in a relationship. It made me sick in the stomach to even think about what a fool I had been. Ed came out of the bathroom, changed and ready. "How do I look?" he asked.

The possibilities of tonight were frightening.

12

REVENGE

Do I smell okay?"

"You smell fine, Ed."

His car jerked into motion, and my head snapped back against the headrest.

"Easy, Ed, we're going to be early as it is."

"Well, I don't want . . . Sharon?" he looked at me to make sure he had her name right, "to get a bad first impression of me."

If you can't say something nice, don't say anything at all.

Ed kept glancing at himself in the rearview mirror. Once he even winked at himself. It was the kind of wink that said, "You're going to do great." I rolled down my window to get some fresh air.

"Whoa, roll it back up! Roll it back up!" Ed screamed.

I rolled it back up. "What's the problem?"

"The wind's going to mess up my hair."

I honestly couldn't resist. "What hair?"

Ed veered to the side of the road and slammed on the

brakes. This time my head bounced off the visor. He glared at me, his face red with anger.

"I don't know why you would say that," he said through clenched teeth. He was purposefully not looking at me as he spoke. "I've told you before, I'm not going bald, I've just got a genetically thin hair pattern."

"I was only joking," I explained. "Your hair looks thick and wavy."

Ed looked hopeful for a moment, as if he believed the compliment. Then he sighed, dropped his shoulders, and slumped over the wheel.

"No, you're right. I'm bald aren't I?"

I thought he was being serious.

"Big deal, Ed, it looks really good on you. I mean it."

"I knew it!" he pointed at my chest. "You really do think I'm bald. What kind of Mormon are you? You beg your roommate to go out with a girl that you are supposed to go out with. Then when you realize that just maybe she is an attractive girl, you decide to make me feel like dirt, hoping that I will bow my genetically thin haired head in defeat and walk away from the situation."

"Ed, what are you talking about?"

"Oh, oh, like you don't know. Well, it's not going to work. I'm in this for the long haul, buddy."

I was speechless. Ed never ceased to amaze me. Such depth and insight. I wanted to be going on this date like I wanted a triple bypass. For him to think that I was trying to make him feel so bad about himself that he would give up and let me have Sharon all to myself was absolutely crazy.

"Ed, I'm not trying to make you feel bad. I think you look

. . . handsome." It was painful to say, it was painful to hear myself say, but Ed seemed to like it.

"What do you mean by handsome?"

I considered opening the door and slamming my head in it.

"I've heard people refer to horses and cabinets as handsome," Ed explained.

"That's what I mean," I said. "Handsome. Like attractive."

In my last three sentences I had used the words *Ed, handsome,* and *attractive.* Something about my life was seriously wrong.

"Attractive like a nice car? Or attractive like someone you would go out with?"

"Ed."

"Well, I need to know."

"Give me a break, Ed."

He pulled back into traffic and we rolled on in momentary silence. I could see that he was still hurt by what I had said and as foolish as it might have been I tried to make him feel better.

"Like someone I would go out with," I said lamely.

"Really?"

I nodded.

"That's great," Ed cheered. "I'll let you in on a little secret. Sometimes when I look in the mirror I see a mighty . . . well, you probably wouldn't care to know."

For once Ed was right.

"When we get back tonight," Ed went on, "I want to show you some of my pictures from high school."

The prospects for tonight kept getting better. A couple of

minutes later we pulled into the apartments. We both got out of the car. I tried to walk a couple of paces behind Ed, but he was determined that we approach the door side by side. So he kept stopping to wait for me to catch up. At the door Ed rang the bell and then put both his arms down to his sides and stood waiting like a stiff robot. The doorknob rattled and then stopped. Quietly the door opened, only to stop when the chain lock had reached its full four-inch length. A pair of green eyes peered out at us.

"Yes?" The mouth below them said.

I knew Ed didn't exactly excel around the opposite sex, so I decided to answer her question. Before I could open my mouth, however, Ed had his up and running. I was amazed at how bold he was.

"Hello, Sister. We are here to see Sharon. Might that be you?"

Might that be you?

"No," she said, closing the door slowly to unhook the chain. She opened it up wide and motioned for us to come in.

"I'll go get her."

"Thanks!" Ed exclaimed. Both the girl and I jumped at the volume of his voice.

We walked in. I sat down on the couch, which was still warm from someone else sitting on it moments before. The TV was on, playing *The Sound of Music*. A large bowl of Chex Mix was sitting on what Ed would call the Postum table. Someone had a nice night at home planned. Ed had both hands in his pockets and was looking closely at all the pictures on the wall.

"I wonder if one of these is Sharon?" he whispered.

I shrugged my shoulders and crossed my legs.

The nuns on TV were wondering how to solve a problem like Maria. Me, I had Ed. The green-eyed girl came back out.

"Sharon is finishing up her hair. She'll be out in a few minutes."

"Great! " Ed said. "And tell me, what is your name?"

"JeanAnn."

"Well, it's a pleasure to meet you, JeanAnn. Isn't that a pretty name?" Ed asked me.

"It sure is," I said. "A lot of N's."

"Thank you," JeanAnn said. "Now if you two don't mind, I'd like to finish watching my movie." She glared at me and the spot I had picked to rest. I jumped up.

"Sorry, I didn't mean to take your place."

She sat down, picked up the Chex Mix, and said nothing more.

JeanAnn was a pretty girl. I couldn't imagine why she was home alone. Sure, her courtesy toward visitors could have used some sprucing up, but she was fairly attractive, which is most likely the reason she was somewhat cold toward us. I knew, however, that the odds of two pretty girls rooming together were pretty slim. There seemed to always be one thin one, one square one, one plain one, and then one that seemed to have the largest amount of what the world would call physical beauty. Ed was in for it—the pretty one had been eliminated.

A figure darted across the hall and hollered, "Just one more minute." I assumed it was Sharon.

"You just take your time," Ed yelled back to an already closed door.

Ed was now doing some serious fidgeting. He kept pulling

the lining of his front pockets out and then shoving them back in while rocking side to side. I leaned in next to him.

"Relax, Ed. It's going to go great."

He didn't answer me, but I could hear him slowly and quietly counting to ten. I tried to think of what to say to Sharon. After all, she expected only me. Thinking of things that I could say to successfully sell Ed was not an easy task.

A door in the hall opened. Ed froze. Out stepped a girl with beautiful red hair and brown eyes. She was tall and made the Chex Mix girl look like a blemish. She was staring straight at Ed.

"Hi. Sharon?" I asked.

"Yes," she answered, never even looking at me.

"My name's—"

"That's nice," she said, cutting me off and still staring at Ed.

Ed moved a step closer and stuck out his hand. "I'm Edward."

"I'm Sharon. Nice to meet you, Edward."

"Are you ready to go?" Ed softly asked.

"Yes," she sighed.

I couldn't believe it. Didn't she realize that Ed was not the person she had talked to on the phone? Ed looked at me.

"Do you mind waiting here until we get back?"

I looked around, suddenly very self-conscious. "I guess not."

JeanAnn stopped eating Chex Mix for a moment, so that she could size me up. The front door slammed and Ed and Sharon were gone.

What had happened? Was this some sort of dating secret combination? Had Ed known Sharon before? What would possess a beautiful girl to walk out alone with Ed after only a few words? Maybe this was just some elaborate ploy to get me alone with this JeanAnn girl.

"I know what you're thinking," JeanAnn said.

"What?"

"I know what you're thinking. You're wondering why someone as beautiful as Sharon would not even notice you and jump out the door with a guy that you, for some reason, think is unattractive."

"I'm not—"

She continued. "You think you are so attractive that you're qualified to judge good looks. You have pity for this, this Ed guy. Because he doesn't look like your concept of handsome."

"Hey," I defended myself. "I just told him in the car that he was handsome. And that—"

She cut me off again.

"I wouldn't even be the least bit surprised if you and your inflated ego thought that this was just one big effort to give me a moment alone with you." She huffed and turned her attention back to the Chex Mix.

What could I say? She was dead on.

"I was a little surprised that they just left," I admitted. "I mean, I feel like my staying here is an imposition to you."

She looked at me, squinted her eyes, and jiggled her head. I think she was mocking me. I could see now why Sharon was having such a rotten time with her roommates. This girl was bitter.

"I'm sorry if I did something to make you mad, I—"

She did what she did best and cut me off again.

"Sit down."

121

I sat.

"Two nights ago my boyfriend, Ryan, told me that it was over between us. Do you understand? I waited two years for him, and when he finally returns he decides that he would like a nineteen-year-old instead of someone who's twenty-two. You know, younger, prettier, and more easily impressed. So, here I sit, eating two-day-old Chex Mix and watching *The Sound of Music* for the hundredth time in my life with some guy who only sees outer beauty." She pressed the mute button on the TV remote control and turned to face me. She looked as if she were expecting some sort of rebuttal.

"Listen, JeanAnn, I'm sorry if I made such a bad first impression. But I'm really not as big a jerk as you might suspect I am. It's completely flattering to know you think that I have some reason to perceive myself as attractive, but I'm as unsure of myself as anyone. I do need to be nicer to Ed, but he can really get on my nerves. You can understand that, can't you? It's not easy being roommates with someone."

"You're right about that," she said, the right corner of her mouth beginning to bend upward.

"I mean, I love the guy, but every night he records his journal entries into a mini dictating machine while pacing the apartment. And he starts each entry by saying, 'Star date,' and then the current day in numbers."

JeanAnn sort of snickered.

"Well, Sharon flosses her teeth every spare moment she has. And if she has to talk on the phone or have a conversation with someone while she is flossing, she just lets the floss hang from her teeth. It's very annoying."

"Hey, even though our apartment manager mows the lawn every two weeks, Ed always goes out and mows the part directly in front of our door. 'We don't want to be known as the messy tenants,' he always says."

JeanAnn was laughing.

"Sharon always tapes off the hall and commands us to stay behind the tape when she's taking a bath. She likes to leave the bathroom door open when she bathes, because she doesn't like it to get all steamy in the bathroom."

"No wonder those two hit it off so well," I said. "They're perfect for each other."

JeanAnn looked at me and then slowly offered me the Chex Mix. Peace had been achieved. Unfortunately, a few miles away a small war was brewing.

13

THERE IS SAFETY IN SILENCE

Bronwyn. What are you doing here?" Ed put down his fork and slid out of the booth he and Sharon were sharing.

"I was at my aunt's here in town talking to my mom. My dad had a mild heart attack tonight."

"Is he all right?" Ed asked with concern.

"I think so. I hope so. I called over to your apartment to try and get hold of Ian, but no one answered. I thought I would come grab something to eat."

"Oh, look at me forgetting my manners," Ed suddenly remembered. "Bronwyn, this is Sharon. Sharon, this is Bronwyn. Bronwyn is my roommate, Ian's, girlfriend," Ed explained.

"Oh," Sharon said back.

"Speaking of Ian, where is he?" Bronwyn asked.

"He's at Sharon's watching a movie with JeanAnn," Ed said without thinking.

"JeanAnn?" Bronwyn asked.

"Yeah, she's Sharon's roommate," Ed went on. "He wanted to watch movies with her."

Sharon nodded, confirming what Ed had just said.

Bronwyn said good-bye and moved out into the now very late night. Ed and Sharon made their third trip to the all-you-can-eat sundae bar, unaware of any damage they might have done.

14

SLOBBER

What time is it?" I asked, confused.

JeanAnn looked at me like I was crazy.

"It's one-thirty," she said. "You fell asleep, and I pushed you onto the floor. I didn't think it would be right for you to sleep on the couch while I was still sitting here."

"Good idea," I said sarcastically. "Where are Ed and Sharon?"

"The only place I know they are not, is here."

I pulled myself slowly off the floor and onto my feet. I could feel the lines that the carpet had made on my face from lying on it. I looked into the mirror on the wall. The left half of my face looked like a ridged potato chip. My hair was sticking up on top, so I tried to smash it down. JeanAnn had on some sort of nightcap on and was wrapped like a mummy in blankets.

"When did I fall asleep?"

"About the time Maria decided to return to the Captain."

"Why didn't you wake me up?"

JeanAnn shrugged her shoulders, "You looked so darn peaceful."

"So you shoved me on the floor?"

"It's not appropriate for you to be sleeping next to me on the—"

"I know," I waved with frustration. "Just tell Ed that I walked home."

"How far do you live?" she asked.

"About five miles from here."

She got up from the couch. "If you wait a minute I'll take you."

"Are you sure?"

"Yeah, I'm sure," she said, lacking the enthusiasm that I felt she should feel and walking back to her room to grab her keys.

The TV was now playing some movie that had far too much singing for my taste. I closed my eyes and tried to ignore it. JeanAnn came back out.

"Come on," she insisted.

I followed her out to a huge rust-colored car. The back bumper was adorned with a sticker that read "America First." The front seat of her car was one long bench. When she adjusted the seat to reach the pedals, it crammed my knees into the dash. I looked over and smiled at her. She was still wearing her nightcap. I wanted to laugh out loud about how ridiculous she looked, but just moments before I had been snoring and drooling on her living room floor—and to the best of my knowledge she had refrained from laughing at me.

We pulled out of her apartment's parking lot.

"Do you want to stop at the Quick-E Mart and get a drink or something?" JeanAnn asked. She had both her hands firmly on the steering wheel. Her left in the eleven o'clock position and her right hand at two. Her arms were completely straight, and she looked as if she were bracing herself for my answer.

"It's sort of late," I hedged.

"I understand," she said stiffly. "If you don't want to be . . ."

Like a fool I took pity. "If you really want to stop and get a drink that would be fine," I conceded.

She didn't say anything, but she slowed and turned down the street that led to the Quick-E Mart. We pulled into the parking lot. The place was deserted—just one lone car sat in the far left parking space. The vehicle obviously belonged to the poor clerk who had to work this late at night.

We got out of the car and JeanAnn pulled off her nightcap. Her hair was neatly braided, and I noticed that she had put some makeup on. Apparently this ride was more important to her than I thought. I felt sort of flattered. I mean, after all she was a beautiful girl, and I had somehow impressed her.

I pulled the Quick-E Mart door open for her.

"Thank you," she said somewhat seductively and louder than I felt was necessary.

"You're welcome," I replied.

The clerk spotted us and spoke up.

"JeanAnn, what are you doing here?" He seemed flustered.

"Oh, Ryan," she said coolly, "I didn't know you were working tonight."

"JeanAnn," he whined. "I told you it was over between the two of us. Margery Sue and I are engaged."

JeanAnn humphed. "For your information, Ryan, I don't care. My boyfriend wanted to stop for a drink and so here we are. I figured you were man enough to be able to deal with it."

"Boyfriend?" I said in confusion.

"Oh, sweety," JeanAnn cooed, brushing my cheek with her hand. "He just loves to tell the world that he's my boyfriend," she explained to Ryan. "He's a doctor," she added.

"I . . ." tried to speak.

"What he's trying to say is that he just got off a twenty-four hour shift at the hospital. How many lives did you save tonight?" she asked me.

I looked at her like she was daft.

"A straight shift sure wears him out," she answered for me. "We best get you home, stat," she joked, poking me in the ribs.

I couldn't believe it. I was a pawn, being used to make an ex-boyfriend jealous. Ryan looked at me with concern.

I scowled, more at the situation than at him.

"Listen, I don't know you," Ryan stuttered nervously. "But I don't want any trouble. Why don't you just take JeanAnn and leave. I'll even give you a soda on the house."

"He doesn't need your money, Ryan," JeanAnn said with a jutted chin. "Perhaps you didn't hear. Ian's a doctor. Since you can't handle seeing me with another guy then I guess we'll just go elsewhere for a drink. Sugar pie," JeanAnn said, offering her arm to me.

I kept my arm to myself.

"Oh, you funny pooh," JeanAnn said, grabbing my arm anyway. "Let's get out of here."

I really didn't want to be anyone's funny pooh, but I did want to get out of there.

Ryan looked greatly relieved at the prospect of us leaving. JeanAnn pulled on my arm. We walked out and got into her car. She hurriedly sped out of the parking lot. I could see Ryan inside calling someone on the phone. Most likely he was phoning Margery Sue to tell her about the whole incident.

"I'm not a doctor," I pointed out as we drove.

"I know that. Which apartments do you live in?" she asked.

I answered.

She pushed on the gas, throwing me back against the bench. She ran two red lights and one stop sign. I was surprised we made it to my place alive.

"Which number?" she barked.

I pointed toward my door.

She pulled up and waited for me to get out. I barely had time to close the car door before she zoomed off. I had forgotten that Ed had the keys, so I was locked out. I thought about waking up the apartment manager and getting him to let me in. But I decided to lay down on the grass and wait for Ed. The sky was so black that it looked purple, and small white stars glowed like fruit from the tree of life. A giant star shot across the sky, causing the glory of those around it to diminish.

I was still upset that Bronwyn had stood me up and that my dating revenge had been such a flop. Bronwyn knew that I was crazy about her. The problem was that she had too much control of this relationship.

After JeanAnn dropped me off, I could hear the phone

ringing in my apartment. It rang six times and then stopped. I looked at my watch. Where was Ed?

A cop car pulled into the parking lot. It crept slowly over to where I was. A bright beam of brilliant light shone down upon me. I blinked and held my hand over my eyes. The siren blurted out two yelps.

"Would you please stand," the cop said over his loud-speaker.

I stood as lights from all the apartments around me came jumping on. It seemed as if my neighbors were as stereo-typically nosy as neighbors tend to be.

"There are loitering laws on the book," the cop said through his speaker.

"I live here."

The cop set down his speaker phone, came out of his car, and sauntered over to me.

"Can you tell me what you're doing lying in the grass at two in the morning?" He sort of wriggled his lips and held tightly onto his Batman-looking cop belt. I recognized him as Bob, the same officer who had helped out at the gas station in Forget many miles and weeks before. What he was doing here was beyond me.

"You look familiar," Bob stared. "I meet a lot of good people, but I also know a lot of folks who have wandered onto the wrong side of the law." I think he was accusing me of something.

"We met at that gas station in Forget a month or so ago."

"Sure," Bob said as if he only half-trusted me.

I decided to explain what I was doing. "I'm locked out and waiting for my roommate to get home. He should be here any moment."

131

The apartment manager came out of his unit and walked over to us.

"What's going on here?" he asked both Bob and me.

I let Bob do the talking.

"Does this person live here?" he asked, pointing toward me.

"He does," my apartment manager confirmed.

"You're sure?"

"I am, he lives right there." He pointed to my door.

"And who are you?" Bob asked.

"I'm the apartment manager."

"Well," Bob said happily. "This works out just right. I'm looking for my nephew. My dear sister sent him up here. He lives in . . . lets see." Bob patted his pockets, searching for something. He pulled a piece of paper from his front pocket. "Oh, this is just my grocery receipt. I save these things," he explained. "If you spend over forty dollars you get a free sandwich." He paused as if contemplating the sandwich.

I cleared my throat in an attempt to bring him back to our conversation.

"Yes," he said dreamily. "Where was I?"

"I have no idea," my apartment manager said, frustrated. "You were looking for a niece or something."

"My nephew," Bob said. "Good kid. He's up here getting a higher education." Bob found another piece of paper in another pocket. "Here it is," he exclaimed. "The Windsor Apartments."

"That's across town," my manager said.

"I'm a stranger to these streets," Bob admitted. "Could you pencil me out a map? I've been driving around for hours.

That's how I happened to see this young man loitering," he pointed at me.

I attempted to explain to both Bob and Bill. "My roommate has my keys, so I was just lying on the grass waiting for him. I didn't want to wake you up, Bill."

"Well, I'm up now, Ian. Me and half the complex."

"I can see you two have issues," Bob said, holding his palms up. "I'll just keep driving around until I find my nephew so as to not cause you any more trouble."

Bob walked backwards slowly. He heaved his big belly into his car and then sped away.

"It makes you feel so safe to have good cops like that around," I joked to Bill.

If he found my remark funny he didn't let on. Bill opened up my apartment, grumbling the whole time about how little he got paid to do what he was having to do. I apologized, but I could tell it did no good.

I got into bed just as Ed returned. I couldn't remember if I had enough cause to be angry at him, so I just pretended to be asleep. He whistled and sang for about half an hour, finally going to sleep around 3:30. Apparently his date had gone well. I fell asleep to the sound of students fixing an early-morning breakfast in the apartment above.

15

AS IF YOU DIDN'T KNOW

So, we wound up talking until two in the morning. Time had no hand in what we were doing. We were like two pieces that had just discovered their missing part." Ed stopped talking to swirl grape jelly onto his toast. He put a corner of the toast into his mouth and bit down, rotated to the next corner, and did the same. He continued until he ended up with just the center, which he stabbed into his now sticky mouth. "I am in love," he announced dreamily.

We were sitting at the kitchen table eating breakfast and discussing last night's festivities.

"That's great, Ed."

"Oh, we saw Bronwyn last night."

"Where?" I asked.

"I guess her dad had a heart attack. She was over at her aunt's house talking to her family. That's why she stood you up. She was in Denny's getting something to eat by herself when we saw her."

"A heart attack! Why didn't you tell me sooner?"

"It was only a mild one," Ed waved. "She said he's all right."

I jumped up from the counter and ran to the phone. I dialed her number wrong twice before I got it right.

"Is Bronwyn there?"

"Yes, just a moment."

A heart attack, glory be. She hadn't stood me up.

"Hello?"

"Hi," I said.

There was an awkward pause.

"Ed just told me about your dad. Is he all right?"

"He's fine, thank you," her voice was sort of cold and distant.

"Well, I was just worried. I hope everything is going to be okay."

"Don't worry about it."

"Is something the matter?" I asked.

"No, but I need to go. I'll talk to you later."

She hung up the phone.

I felt like someone had taken a wood plane to my heart. I had never heard Bronwyn like this before.

"What's up?" Ed asked as I walked back into the kitchen looking worried.

"I don't know. Bronwyn was acting kind of funny."

"She was acting funny last night, too."

"What did she say?"

"Not much. She asked about you, and we told her you were with JeanAnn. Then she said good-bye and just walked off."

I put my hands in my head and moaned, "Ed."

"Women," he said flippantly. "Who can read 'em?"

135

Fifteen minutes later I was standing on Bronwyn's doorstep, flowers in hand, and a small amount of hope in heart. She answered the door.

"What are you doing here?" she asked, looking almost happy to see me.

"I came to clear something up."

"There's nothing to clear up, Ian."

I dived in. "You're mad at me because you think I went out with someone else last night," I offered. "Well, it's sort of true. I thought you stood me up, and I had been thinking a lot about this dating game, and what my home evening group had said. So like an idiot, I called this girl in my marriage prep class to see if she wanted to go out with me. But I dialed the wrong number and accidentally asked out a stranger, before I got a chance to realize what I was doing. So, I asked Ed to take her out instead of me because I really didn't want to go out with anyone except you anyway. Ed said yes, but only if I would go with them. I consented, but when we got over there Ed and this Sharon girl had some sort of love at first sight thing going on and left me at home with Sharon's bitter roommate, JeanAnn. Well, we didn't do anything except watch *The Sound of Music,* and I fell asleep on the floor. When I woke up it was one-thirty, so I decided to walk home, but JeanAnn insisted on driving me and then made me visit some ex-boyfriend of hers on the way. When we finally got to my place I was locked out, so I had to wait on the grass till Ed got home. Then a cop named Bob hassled me. That's the truth. I'm sorry about attempting to ask someone else out. But I really thought you had stood me up, and I was confused, and I didn't know what to do. And keep in mind that I am a male, and these type of mix-ups are sort of in our blood. Can you ever forgive me?" I took a deep breath and held out the flowers to her.

"So, who is this girl in your marriage prep class?" she asked.

"Bronwyn, will you forgive me?" I answered.

"I'll think about it," she took the flowers and then went back into her apartment and closed the door.

I drove home and waited by the phone for a formal acceptance of my apology. Three hours later I finally called her and talked her into forgiving me. It took some finagling, but I felt she was sincere.

16

HARD-BOILED

Ed had many quirks that were both bothersome and hard to live with. He talked too much, sang too much, and was constantly referring to Bolivia or butting into my business. But he did have some good points—okay, one good point. His parents owned a condo in California, and he had permission to use it whenever he wanted to. After much pestering and persuading I finally talked him into taking Sharon, Bronwyn, and me to the condo for a vacation and school getaway.

We threw our suitcases into Ed's car and jumped in. Bronwyn and Sharon were ready and waiting when we picked them up, which saved us from missing our flight. We got to our plane just as they were closing the doors. We found our seats and jammed our belongings into the overhead compartments.

We were not in the air more than fifteen minutes before the stewardess started coming down the aisle, passing out snacks. She gave us our packet of peanuts and a small cup of pop, then moved on to the people behind us. We all dived into our tiny portions of peanuts as if we hadn't eaten for days.

"I wish we were flying long enough to get a movie," Ed said.

"Oh, Ed," Sharon laughed as if he had just told a joke. Ed smiled and patted her on the knee.

Bronwyn rolled her eyes at me, then whispered in my ear.

"No secrets," Ed said loudly. "If you're going to say something, you have to share it with all of us."

"Those are the rules," Sharon added.

"Rules?" Bronwyn asked. "I didn't know there were any rules."

"Oh, yes," Ed said authoritatively. "Sharon and I wrote down a list of rules for the trip, and no secrets is one of them."

"That's great, Ed, but your rules do not apply to us," I said.

"Ed's condo, Ed's rules," Ed said.

Sharon nodded her head in agreement. Ed turned to look out the window, and Bronwyn accidentally threw a honey-roasted peanut at the back of his head.

"Hey! No throwing things, that's rule number seven," he said.

"Maybe you should read us these rules, Ed. So we don't accidentally break any more of them," I said.

Ed pulled a neatly folded piece of paper from his shirt pocket. "California Trip Rules: Number One: Always stick together. Number Two: Don't count money in the open. Number Three: Be suspicious of everyone. Number Four: Keep no secrets from one another."

Ed paused to look our way. He then continued, "Number Five: Split costs evenly.

"Number Six: Respect my parents' property. Number Seven: No throwing anything."

Another pause and a slight nod in our direction.

"Number Eight: Keep our tempers in check. Number Nine: Watch out for each other. And Number Ten is: Respect the proper chain of command."

Ed folded the paper and put it back in his pocket.

Bronwyn couldn't help it, she began to laugh. A few other passengers who had heard the list were laughing as well.

"Well," Ed huffed, pulling out his list again. "I guess I'll have to add no laughing."

That made me laugh.

Ed threw his arms up in the air, disgusted by our lack of respect. He grabbed Sharon's hand, and the two of them stormed off to some empty seats at the back of the plane. We didn't see either of them again until the plane landed.

"Sorry, Ed," I said, as we were retrieving our things from the overhead bins. He didn't answer. He and Sharon waited for Bronwyn and me to get our stuff out; then they followed us off the plane and down the ramp.

We had no luggage except for our carry-ons, so we all went straight to the rent-a-car desk and got the keys to our car. It was raining hard, and the clouds above looked too thick to ever move on. Ed and Sharon still were not saying anything. Even when I asked him if he wanted to drive, he just stuck his chin out and remained silent.

"Ed, I have no idea where to go, or how to get there, so you probably should be the one to drive."

He took the keys from me, opened Sharon's door for her, and then got into the driver's seat.

"Ed, I'm sorry I laughed," Bronwyn said, sounding genuinely apologetic. "It's just that some of the things on the list are kind of . . . funny."

Ed started the engine and relaxed his shoulders. "If you remember Rule Number Ten, which is to respect the proper chain of command, then you would understand why it is crucial for you to not laugh at what I suggest."

I could only take so much from Ed. After all, he was my roommate, and I was *supposed* to disagree and fight with him, at least ninety percent of the time.

"What the heck is the proper chain of command?"

"Well, it's my parents' condo, so I am first in command. Sharon, being my girl, is second; Ian, you're third; and Bronwyn is fourth."

"Thanks for including me," Bronwyn said flatly.

"If we all stick to the rules, a good time will be had by all," was Ed's closing argument.

I wanted to say something more and perhaps even do a little name-calling, but Bronwyn was digging her nails into my knee, indicating that I should remain silent. So, I did.

We had all mellowed by the time we reached Ed's parents' condo. It was a beautiful place, surrounded by palm trees and flowers and right on the beach. The waves washing up on the sand and the smell of salt hanging in the misty air made the setting even more appealing.

Ed turned off the car and we all got out. The sound of the ocean and the seabirds made me wish it wasn't raining.

"Not bad," I said to Bronwyn.

"Not at all," she said, taking my hand.

Suddenly from the direction of the condo came a noise. Not a normal noise, but a high-pitched squeal, like someone backing over a howler monkey.

"What is that?" I asked.

"Must be a fire engine or something," Bronwyn answered.

If only she had been right. Descending the condo steps at a speed that only a leopard could approach was a woman who looked to be in her mid-sixties. Her dyed-red hair was stuck to her head from the rain, and she was flailing her arms wildly above her head. She had on shorts that came just below her knees and enough jewelry around her neck to make even the Pope contemplate robbery.

"Eddie! Eddie!" she was screaming. She bounded into Ed's arms, and he embraced her tightly. Their floral shirts seemed to mesh into one.

"Who is that?" Bronwyn whispered.

I was about to remind her about the no secrets rule when Ed waved us over.

"Everybody, this is Aunt Nanny. Aunt Nanny, this is everybody." Ed opened both his arms toward us as if he were a game-show girl showing us a new TV.

Sharon shook Aunt Nanny's hand; Bronwyn and I just nodded.

"Eddie!" Aunt Nanny gushed. "I was so thrilled when you invited your uncle and me to spend the weekend with you and your school friends. Your uncle's been so sick and all with the sores and swelling. This weekend will do him a world of good. Of course we forgot his ointment, but . . ." She paused for breath and then looked at Bronwyn and me. "What am I doing? Let's all get in there and see your parents, Eddie. We've been waiting all day for you."

What was happening? Surely Ed's aunt, uncle, and parents were not sharing the condo with us? I must have heard wrong when Ed's aunt had said that Ed had invited them here this weekend.

"Ed, can I talk to you?" I asked.

"In a moment," Ed said, running up the stairs with Sharon.

Bronwyn looked at me as if she had just heard that someone dear to her had passed away. "I didn't realize that we were sharing the place with others," she said. "I thought it was just going to be us four," she said.

"Same here."

We walked slowly up the steps and into the condo. It was a great place, but it was slightly cluttered with people at the moment. Ed was hugging an older woman who looked just like him—I assumed it was his mom. There was a tall, older man in a floral shirt, with a thick head of hair, standing next to the fireplace. He, too, looked like Ed, except for the hair.

"Come in, Ian," Ed said. "Mom, Dad, this is my roommate, Ian, and his girlfriend, Bronwyn."

"Bronwyn?" Ed's Mom said, cocking her head. "Interesting name, what is it, Hawaiian?"

"Actually it's Welsh," Bronwyn said.

"Hawaiian, Welsh, no matter," the thick-haired man broke in. "I'm Ed's father, and around here we're all American."

I sat down, despondent and disheartened. This was not going to be the weekend I had envisioned. Ed's parents pointed out the rooms each of us would be staying in and then sent us down the hall to unpack.

"Ed, you never said a thing about your entire family tree spending the weekend with us," I said as soon as he and I were alone in our room. I was trying hard not to sound completely devastated by what was happening.

"I thought this would be an ideal time for Sharon to meet my family. Besides, it's always more fun with family around."

"I thought your parents lived in Maine," I said, frustrated.

"They do," Ed said. "They flew out just for this weekend, so if you could please not ruin it for them I would appreciate it."

"You could have told me," I said rubbing my forehead.

"I thought you liked surprises."

"Pleasant surprises, yes."

Ed unpacked the few things he had brought and put them into the large wardrobe in our room. I wanted to bludgeon him with my small bag, but I didn't. I unloaded my stuff into the cherry-wood dresser and went to look for Bronwyn.

She was helping Ed's mom peel hard-boiled eggs in the kitchen sink.

"Can I help?" I asked, hoping they would say no.

"Sure," Ed's mom said, handing me a basket of eggs. "We're all going to take a road trip tomorrow, and I thought that a good supply of hard-boiled eggs would be a welcome treat to a van full of hungry sightseers."

I hated hard-boiled eggs: I hated the smell, I hated the texture, and I hated the taste. But because I couldn't say no, my hands and the hands of the girl I loved were soon wrist deep in the rubbery things—cracking and peeling them by the dozen. And all in preparation for some sure-to-be-unforgettable road trip we were supposed to take tomorrow. Memories of family outings from years gone by sizzled on my poached brain. We had been forced to eat hard-boiled eggs and drink ordinary tap water from a thermos on our family trips, while all my friends got to eat at McDonald's and convenience stores on theirs.

"Think of all the money we're saving," my mother would say, as if it would actually make the eggs taste better.

I used to stuff my coat pockets full of eggs until I could get to a toilet and flush them. I didn't mind going hungry as long as I didn't have to feel those eggs coating my teeth and tongue.

Ed came into the kitchen and gave his mother another hug.

"Umm. Eggs," he said, licking his lips.

"I can't believe Ed's family is here," Bronwyn whispered as we stood side by side, surrounded by whites and yolks.

"I can't either," I whispered back. "But when we get home, if we get home that is, I'm never going to let Ed live this down. He invited them all without ever saying a thing to me about it." I squeezed an egg in my hand and watched and felt it ooze through my frustrated fingers.

"What are you two talking about?" Ed asked suspiciously.

"Nothing," I snapped.

He ignored my quick response and went out into the living room to greet his Uncle Myron, who had just gotten back from picking up some nonprescription painkillers for himself. I washed my hands, and Bronwyn and I slipped out the back door and toward the beach before we could be assigned some other disgusting task.

A warm, misty rain was coming down lightly, adding to the beauty of the surrounding ocean. We walked hand in hand, breathing in the salty air and moist breeze.

"Looks like it's going to be one really weird weekend," I said.

"Amen to that," Bronwyn said.

We stopped and wrote our names in the wet sand, then tried to find shells that looked unusual enough to keep. We had taken off our shoes, and Bronwyn's feet looked so cute speckled with sand that I felt compelled to comment on it.

"You're really strange," she said in response.

I guess my feet didn't look cute enough for her to mention.

The longer we were out there, the deeper we allowed ourselves to wade into the water. First it was our feet, then our ankles. Our knees were only under the water two minutes before we were wet to our waists. It was inevitable—we ended up swimming in the rain. It was cold, both in the water and out, but we ignored it and swam and played our way down the shore until we were at least a mile away from Ed's condo and family center.

"Maybe we should head back," Bronwyn said.

I made fun of her for sounding like my mom, and we continued what we were doing for at least another mile more.

"Maybe we should head back now," I said.

Of course Bronwyn never listened to me, so we goofed around for about a half mile more. The sky now looked very dark and the rain was coming down much harder. We were both shivering.

"Now?" I asked.

Bronwyn nodded in agreement.

Going back wasn't as much fun.

"Do you like eggs?" I asked Bronwyn as we walked.

"They're all right, why?"

"Well, the way I see it is that they are sort of like bananas. I like dried bananas, banana creme pie, and banana flavored candy. But I can't stand the real thing, something about the texture." I shuddered for effect. "It's the same way with eggs: I like them scrambled until they're dry, or in macaroni salad, if they're chopped real fine, but other than that, I hate them."

"I'm impressed with how much thought you've put into your eggs," Bronwyn said sarcastically.

"I just don't want you to ever go to the trouble of fixing me a hard-boiled egg and then expect me to eat it."

"Don't worry, I'll never go to the trouble," she said. "Can we talk about something besides eggs now?" Bronwyn asked.

I guess she must have taken my walking hand in hand with her and looking content as a yes because she continued talking.

"What do you think of our relationship? And no stupid answers, I really want to know."

"I think it's the greatest. This is what I have wanted my whole life, and now it's coming to pass. I can't tell you how devastated I was when I heard you had married Brian. I felt like my life was ruined. I know it was wishful thinking on my part, but I just wanted one chance for you to get to know me. I remember that I used to fantasize about you having a secret fan club for me. I could imagine you and your friends gathering in the school restroom, secretly talking about me and how much you wished you could get to know me. Of course you could never actually say anything to me because, heck, that would ruin the purpose of a secret fan club. It helped me feel better each time you just walked past me without saying hi, or at all the church functions when you and your friends would run off and do things with the older boys."

"Secret fan club, huh?"

"Yep," I said.

"Well, do you want to know what I thought about you?"

"I guess, but don't be too mean," I said, picking up a broken seashell and tossing it into the ocean.

Bronwyn put her hand in mine and used the other to wipe some of the rain from her eyes.

"I always thought you were really smart," she said. "I think it was because you didn't hang around with anybody extremely cool. I liked you all through fifth grade, but I never let on to it. I didn't want anyone to know that I liked them because my mom always said that the moment boys think you like them, that's when they will start to act crazy. I guess she was right. I thought I liked Brian, but as soon as I began to show it, he turned into a different person—and he went beyond crazy. Now, I think I'm starting to really like you, and, well, you're starting to bring up things like eggs as topics of conversation." She smiled.

"A definite pattern," I said.

It was now dark, and we could see some people with flashlights walking toward us on the beach. The way their flashlights seemed to search the shore indicated that they were looking for something.

We moved closer to them. It was Ed and his family. When they saw us they ran toward us, waving their lights and yelling.

"Where have you guys been?" Ed demanded.

"We just took a walk down the beach," I answered.

"Well, don't you ever do that to us again," Ed said.

"Sorry, Ed, I didn't mean—"

He cut me off, "Sorry doesn't cut it. Now you and

Bronwyn have ruined the night for the rest of us. I want you two to stay in the condo unless you clear it with me or my father."

What was this? A direct order from Ed? I'm not hot tempered. No quick reactions or flying off the handle from me. But Ed was picking a fight with me at just the wrong time. I had officially had enough of him. I dug my toes into the sand to vent some frustration and try to calm myself down.

"Back home and inside, the both of you," Ed commanded, pointing.

That was it; I had had enough. "Drop it, Ed."

"Don't tell me what to do," he hollered. "You're third in command and will speak when called upon."

Ed had flipped out.

"Don't pull that chain of command thing on me. Bronwyn and I will do as we please this weekend. And we're going to try and salvage some fun out of it, despite the fact that we have to drag around some sort of family reunion with us."

Ed pushed me.

I pushed him.

He pushed me again.

I jumped on him. We rolled across the sand and into the water. He was no match. In fact he started to scream mercy after only a minute. I let him go and stood up. Bronwyn was laughing. Sharon looked on horrified. And Ed's parents didn't know how to act. His father seemed embarrassed that Ed had begged for mercy, and his mother looked bothered— as if she could foresee the future and the mess we would all make, dripping through the condo. I didn't feel anything besides complete embarrassment. I took Brownwyn's hand and we walked off, toward the condo.

"He gets kind of bossy sometimes," Ed's dad hollered as we walked away.

We had gone a good four-tenths of a mile before Bronwyn finally spoke.

"You two looked so stupid, fighting like that," she laughed.

Great, she was unimpressed with my fighting abilities. I had defended our ground while she picked out another lot of land. This weekend stunk. I could have been home reading or sleeping, but instead I was stuck in California with an assortment of people that the heavens themselves couldn't fancy and a girlfriend who was laughing at me. Plus, I had lost my temper. It seemed that every time I lost my temper I threw my whole being out of whack. People appeared hostile and dumpy and life looked long and painful.

"Let's just go home," I moaned.

"Come on," Bronwyn said. "You're not going to let Ed ruin this weekend for us, are you? Just forget him and let's have a good time."

"I can't just forget him," I complained. "Especially when I know that we're supposed to go on a road trip tomorrow and we're bringing nothing to eat except those eggs."

I had slipped nicely into my martyr complex. The whole world would feel sorry for me before I cheered up. I wanted compensation, I needed vindication, and I demanded retribution. Bronwyn gave me all three.

"I'll tell you what," she said. "Tomorrow, you and I will ditch the road trip and go someplace all by ourselves. And we'll eat nothing but pizza and drink nothing but sodas, okay?"

"Well, I don't—" I began to say.

"Then after that, we'll go out to some fancy restaurant and I can tell you by candlelight that I love you." Bronwyn pulled her wet hair back and tried to twist out some of the water. She looked at me slyly out of the corner of her eye and gave me a grin.

I stopped in my tracks.

I couldn't believe it.

I was speechless.

What I should have done was tell Bronwyn that I loved her back. But all I did was smile at her.

"Are you smiling because I love you, or because you don't have to eat eggs tomorrow?" Bronwyn asked.

My smile doubled—I had forgotten about the eggs.

We had been standing still long enough for Ed and his loved ones to catch up to us. Ed's dad approached me.

"Ian, Ed has something he would like to say to you."

Ed and I walked off away from everyone else.

"I'm sorry about all this, Ian," Ed said apologetically. "I just wanted my dad to see that I'm in control. I guess I blew it."

"Bronwyn loves me," was my only reply.

Ed stared at me blankly.

"She loves me, Ed."

He patted me on the back. "So, I'm forgiven?"

I nodded and we rejoined the others for the walk back.

The condo smelled of eggs when we returned. Ed's mom made us all dinner. We then sat around listening to Uncle Myron tell us about the good old days until late in the night. I sat and watched everyone drop off to sleep as Uncle Myron prattled on. Ed's mom was the first to go, then Sharon, Aunt Nanny, Ed, Bronwyn, and finally Ed's father. It was just Myron and me now, surrounded by a ring of snoring family and friends.

"Guess everyone's heard enough about the good old days for one night," Myron said to me.

"I guess so," I replied.

"She's a beautiful girl," Myron whispered hoarsely.

"Bronwyn?" I asked.

"Yes. Do you plan on marrying her?"

"I hope so," I said quietly.

"Have you written that hope down?"

"Over a million times, I'm sure."

He laughed at me.

"You see Nanny over there?" he said, pointing.

I looked over at her. She lay opened-mouthed, slumped against the back of the couch. She had changed out of her wet clothes into an adult-sized pink sleeper with enclosed feet and was snoring louder than any of the others.

"I met her at a youth function," he continued. "The second I saw her I knew she would be my wife someday. Well, my mother always told me that a goal not written down is just a wish. So, I ran home that night and filled a whole notepad with one goal written over and over again. I still remember the exact wording: 'I will make Nannette Bendermyer my wife or die in the process.'" Myron popped open a bottle of medicine and swallowed a few pills. "Hard to imagine that was her and me all those years ago; things sure do change."

Ed, who had been talking in his sleep the last few minutes, said something that resembled the word *parsley* and then turned over and shut up.

152

"So, how long have you and Ed been rooming together?" Myron asked me.

"Just this semester."

"He's kind of an odd kid, don't you agree?"

I laughed and nodded yes.

"I remember right after he came off his mission. He had fallen madly in love with some beautiful Spanish girl named Maria. He brought her back to the States and they made plans to be married. But she left him for the guy who sold them their wedding announcements. It killed Ed, and he withdrew into himself for a whole year. He never talks about it; in fact he acts like it never happened. The really sad thing is that everyone sort of took Maria's side because Ed is just so hard to live with."

"Sharon sure likes him," I said.

"She's a real charitable girl."

Myron closed his eyes and leaned back in his chair. He opened them a few moments later and acted surprised that I was still there.

"Don't you have something to go write down?" he asked.

"You mean about Bronwyn?"

He nodded his long head.

"I told you that I've already written it down in so many ways."

"I hope you worded it correctly," he said, closing his eyes again and slipping into a medicated sleep.

I woke Bronwyn and said good night to her. She shuffled off to her room still half asleep. I sat there alone for a few minutes, then got up and went to my room. I wrote down my goal three times and then dozed off myself.

17

NOTHING LOOKS THE SAME IN THE LIGHT

I think the beach is at its best in the morning. Most people are still asleep, and you have a full day to enjoy the beauty of it. I had always thought that, as depressing as it must have been to be Adam and Eve—and to have been kicked out of the Garden of Eden—if they wandered far enough, somewhere, they would have come to a beach. That would have had to lift their spirits some.

Bronwyn and I ran down to a local doughnut hut and picked up two dozen doughnuts for everyone's breakfast.

"So, what time did Uncle Myron finally drop off?" Bronwyn asked as we drove.

"I'm not sure," I answered. "I went to bed about eleven, right after you left."

"Were you the only one still awake?"

"Yes."

"Did you two talk?" she asked.

"A little," I said, honking the horn at some birds in the road.

"What did you talk about?"

"Not much. He asked me about you and talked about his wife a little."

Bronwyn flipped down the visor in the rented car and looked at herself in the small mirror. She pushed on the skin under her blue eyes and complained about how bad she looked.

"You look perfect," I insisted.

"That's what I wanted to hear," she said flipping the visor back up. "Let's go park on the beach and eat our doughnuts alone."

We parked and watched two teenage surfers try to keep their balance long enough to ride a full wave—the whole time we were there neither one was successful. The dough-nuts we had bought were powdered on the outside and gave Bronwyn and me white lips.

"It's kind of nice to watch a sunrise and eat doughnuts without having to think of anything else," Bronwyn commented, starting in on her second doughnut.

"What else is there to think about?" I asked.

"You know, school, our fathers' work," she answered, confident that I knew.

"So, do you ever think that our fathers might really be guilty?" I quickly tried to explain myself. "I mean, doesn't it sometimes cross your mind that just maybe they might have been involved? I know my dad's innocent, but sometimes just for a moment I see or hear him do something that makes me suspect that he did do something wrong." I bit into a chocolate-filled doughnut and the filling dropped out onto the seat. I took a napkin and wiped it as clean as possible.

"It doesn't seem possible that either of our fathers could have done anything wrong."

"I'll just be glad when this whole thing is behind us," I chewed. "So I can spend time thinking about other things."

"Like doughnuts and sunrises?" she asked.

"Exactly."

We drove the rest of the doughnuts home to Ed and his bloodline. They inhaled them quickly and without thanks. Ed did get out his pocket calorie counter and read to all of us the contents of doughnuts, pointing out just how horrible they were for us.

Ed's family refused to go on the road trip without Bronwyn and me, so we were forced to give in and go along. I whined accordingly. Ed's parents had rented a huge van for the day, so we all crammed in and were off. Mitchell, Ed's father, kept pointing out obscure buildings and reciting histories no one cared about. At about noon, Ed's mom passed out the hard-boiled eggs, and Bronwyn and I both passed them up. For the next half hour everyone talked with egg bits flying out of their mouths. Their teeth all made a sticky sound as they chewed and swallowed.

Ed's mom did bring red punch instead of just plain water. A small comfort, but at least the smell of the punch helped cover that of the eggs. After drinking we all had big red mustaches. Aunt Nanny looked like Ronald McDonald before he knew how to evenly apply his lipstick.

After a long drive we stopped at a beautiful beach that didn't look much different from the one we had started out from. After staring at it for about thirty minutes we got back in the van and headed home. I volunteered to drive so that the others could talk in the back. Ed's dad jumped at the offer. Bronwyn sat up by me so that we could have our own conversation. We talked and munched on gas station food as the others talked about things I was happy to be excluded from. The shore ran alongside us like blue yarn being quickly unraveled.

"I wish that we lived closer to the ocean," I said. "My land would look so much better with a shore on one of its edges."

"I dreamed about your land last night," Bronwyn remembered. "It wasn't actually your land, though. I think it was some island in Canada."

"Really?" I said.

"It made sense in my dream. Anyhow, we kept picking coconuts and stacking them in large pile. Ed was there. He had long set hair and kept wanting to tell me something."

"What?" I asked.

"I woke up before he could tell me. Weird. I wonder what it means?" she asked herself, handing me some beef jerky.

"Ask Ed," I said. "I think he has a dream interpreting book."

"That's okay," Bronwyn insisted.

"You know," I said, changing the subject. "I think that heaven will be surrounded by beaches. I heard somewhere that Joseph Smith said the City of Enoch was lifted up from the Gulf of Mexico. That would make most of Zion beachfront property. Right?" I asked.

"I think I like it better when you talk about eggs."

"Most people do."

Bronwyn handed me the rest of the food we had bought and then turned away and closed her eyes as if to take a nap. The rest of the drive home was uneventful and lonely. Only once, when I almost hit a dog, did I even feel like I was doing anything.

Bronwyn and I ordered pizza that evening and stayed at

the condo while everyone else went out for Chinese. When they returned we played a few board games and then made brownies. We watched Uncle Myron do a few pathetic magic tricks and listened while Aunt Nanny played a couple of unrecognizable songs on her guitar. I was glad when I was finally able to go to sleep. I dreamt about a field that night, an empty field with a well in the middle, on an island.

We got to the airport early the next morning. Due to some other canceled flights, ours was crowded and disorganized, with people trying to get on to it at the last minute. Bronwyn took the window seat this time, allowing me to stretch my right leg out. They gave us a breakfast as we flew. I should have expected the hard-boiled eggs and ham we were served.

"Eat it," Bronwyn teased.

"No way."

"Just eat it," Ed said, butting into our business.

"No way," I said again.

"Eggs are really good for your hair. They make it shiny and healthy," Sharon informed me.

"Then my hair can eat it," I said defensively.

"What would it take to get you to eat it?" Bronwyn asked.

"I will not eat it," I said, sounding like Sam-I-Am.

"Not even if I asked you to?" Bronwyn teased.

"Not even if you begged me to," I insisted.

A man sitting behind us in his midthirties, with obviously too little to think about, spoke up.

"I'll give you ten bucks if you eat it."

"Count me in," the woman sitting next to him said, pulling out a ten-dollar bill from her purse.

I started to panic.

"I'm not eating this egg," I said, looking down at my tray.

Bronwyn had pushed her egg onto my plate when I wasn't looking. So there were now two eggs staring back at me from my dish.

"Take it back," I said to her, not wanting to touch it myself.

"Eat it, eat it!" everyone chanted.

Bronwyn cut one of the eggs in half with her fork. The yoke, although hard-boiled, dripped some watery substance onto the plate. I felt light-headed.

"Just eat half," Bronwyn said.

"Just half," everyone chanted.

"Does he still get the money if he eats only half?" Ed asked the man and woman behind us.

They nodded yes.

Bronwyn grabbed my arm and told me how impressed she would be if I ate it. She pointed out what a romantic gesture it would be. It would prove that there was nothing I wouldn't do for her. She was joking, but I was dead serious about not eating it. People all around us started popping eggs into their mouths to prove how harmless they were. All that egg breath didn't help.

"Just do it," Ed said.

"Do it, do it," everyone chanted.

I couldn't take it any longer. I was a person of reasonable intellect and this was something that I could end with just one bite. I picked up the egg. I looked at it from all sides. I squeezed it a little and then shoved it in my mouth and swallowed. Bronwyn gasped out of amazement, and the crowd went wild. I would rather have swallowed some rough-grade, soggy sandpaper, but I got it down.

"There," I choked. "Are you all happy now?"

I looked over at Bronwyn, hoping for some kind words, or at least a suggestion of how brave I was.

"Don't breathe over here," she said. "Your breath smells like egg."

The stewardess started back up the aisle to collect the finished meals. I was relieved when the other egg-and-a-half were finally gone. The two passengers paid up even though I told them it wasn't necessary. We landed, disembarked, and drove home.

The scrambled weekend had ended, and two days later when I took Bronwyn out to dinner with the twenty bucks I had made, the egg memories seemed far less painful than they had actually been.

18

CARNIVAL

The clouds picked at each other and then, like loose cotton, broke off and drifted away. I could see the cool in the air and feel the cold in the ground. But my left hand burned as it held onto Bronwyn's right. A small kid with a huge head ran across the path in front of us. He tripped on a stone and fell to the ground. The excitement of the game he was playing made what would normally be a tragic accident go almost unnoticed.

Who would have ever guessed that Bronwyn and I would end up being an item?

We had been seeing each other almost every night for the last two months. I would love to go on and on about the wacky and romantic times we had enjoyed, but in all honesty, it wasn't like that—a fact that I'm quite happy about. We just worked, and it was heavenly, or divine, or perfect— well, it was very nice. At the moment, we were walking around the campus, looking very much like a couple that didn't have anything else to do.

"The carnival will be here in a couple of weeks," Bronwyn

said as we passed a poster plastered to a street post. "Do you want to go?"

"Sure, I guess."

"We don't have to go if you don't want to."

"I said sure."

"I know, but the way you said it . . ." Bronwyn pinched the skin between my thumb and index finger on the hand she was holding. I felt obliged to say ouch.

"So, if you don't want to go—"

"I want to go," I insisted.

"How about the first Friday it's here?"

I nodded in agreement and then pinched her back. Her ouch was much more sincere than mine.

19

TAKING COUNSEL

I was at my wit's end. I had prayed about it and the answer I seemed to have gotten was, yes. Yes, I should marry her? Or yes, I should come to my senses and realize that a girl like that could never be eternally happy with a guy like me? I thought seriously about calling my dad for help. But as much as I loved him, I just couldn't bear to hear him tell me, "Seasons, my son, seasons. There is a season for this and a season for that. And this is that season for this."

His intentions would be good, but his knack for glossing things over would prevail. So, I turned to the only person I thought of who could really help—my marriage prep teacher.

"Ian Smith, right?"

"That's right," I said, as my professor sat down behind his desk. I took a seat beside it.

"What is it that I can help you with?"

"Well, I think I just might have found that one person for me. Now what?"

"Have you prayed about it?"

"Yes."

"And your answer?"

"Positive."

"Well, then, what's the problem?" He tugged and brushed the sleeve of his burlap-looking sports coat. He was treating my contemplation of marriage as some sort of normalcy.

"So, what you're saying is that if I've received a positive answer in prayer, this is green light enough to ask this girl to marry me?" I felt I should add, "We're not talking a civil marriage; this would definitely take place in the temple." Just in case he was thinking that this was only until death.

He picked up his brown Bible and began flipping through the pages.

"It's no use," I said forlornly. "I've read every scripture on marriage referenced in the Topical Guide, and there are over three full pages of them. None of them moved me to the point of feeling comfortable with finalizing my celestial choice. Besides, the way I see it is that it really isn't up to me. It's up to her. Will she accept me? Does she truly want kids that somewhat resemble me? When I tell our children to go to bed, will she turn around and say, 'You kids can stay up. Don't listen to your mean father.' My brother says marriage is like a grapefruit—bigger than an orange, but not half as sweet. What is that supposed to mean? Are there some marriage secrets that you are told only after you are married? I guess what I really want to know is, can I honestly trust myself to make this kind of decision?" I exhaled loudly.

"It sounds to me like you're making this situation so uncomfortable that no one could possibly accept it. Do you love her?" he asked.

I gave him my most enthusiastic nod.

"Does she love you?"

I felt like we were two young girls sharing secrets at a slumber party.

"Yes," I giggled.

"There you have it. Don't put a curse on this thing called marriage just because of your brother's grapefruit theory. And if she says yes, which I have a feeling she will, then she obviously loves you. And ten to one, she's already thought about how your future kids will look." He focused in on his scriptures. "Second Kings, chapter two, verses twenty-three and twenty-four. Do you remember Elisha?"

I remembered, I just wasn't sure who he or she was.

He began reading: "And he went up from thence unto Beth-el: and as he was going up by the way, there came forth little children out of the city, and mocked him, and said unto him, Go up, thou bald head; go up, thou bald head.

"And he turned back, and looked on them, and cursed them in the name of the Lord. And there came forth two she bears out of the wood, and tare forty and two children of them."

"So marriage will make me bald?" I tried to understand.

He waved my remark off. "Let's change it a little," he said, making me feel like I was back in grade school.

"And he left his marriage prep class and went unto the real world. And as he began going the way of the world, there came forth people with little knowledge, truly youngsters in the ways of the Lord. And they mocked him, saying things like, marriage can wait, you couldn't live with this person forever, go up and date much more. And he turned back and looked on them. And he cursed them, saying shame on you. Marriage is a celestial institution. And the Lord sent two single males between the age of thirty-five and forty to talk

165

their ears off. And they talked the ears off forty and two of them."

My teacher sat back in his chair and folded his arms and smiled. He was acting as if this little story would clear up everything for me. But all it did was make me doubt my decision to come to him for help. I stared at him blankly. Was I supposed to laugh or just keep nodding as if I understood the deeper wisdom of the story?

"The moral of the story," he finally said, "is that you know what to do. Don't let any outside forces or unknowing beings make up your mind. Marriage is good."

Now he was making a bit of sense. Bronwyn was a beautiful girl, and the idea of us being husband and wife didn't seem to turn her stomach. It's just that all your life you seem to live to get married, and now that that time was finally here I was unsure of myself. The commitment didn't scare me, but I had a history of clumsily stumbling through important decisions in my life. And I insisted that this decision be made differently.

"Professor," I asked, hoping my question wouldn't provoke another story. "Do you think that you could be married to *anyone* and make it work if you had the drive to do so?"

"Well, if you had the patience and compassion it could work. Many arranged marriages work, and many fail. Depends on the respect and effort put into it."

I figured that if two people who were forced to be together could make it work, then certainly two people as happy with each other as Bronwyn and I were with one another could make miracles.

"Thanks, Professor," I said, getting up and leaving the room.

I was going to do it. Not because of the scriptures he had read or because of all the righteous, well-meaning advice I had gotten lately. I would do it because she was Bronwyn and I was Ian—the combination was correct. I was a little too literal sometimes.

The veil thinned, and the angels whooped as I walked back to my apartment. The decision had been made.

20

FERRIS

The wheels had been set in motion. We would spend the afternoon at the carnival and the evening enjoying dinner by candlelight, then finish the night by driving up into the mountains above the city. Then, and only then, would I ask her the question and wait for the reply. Not incredibly original, but it was a recipe that had worked for many love-struck couples—why not us?

"Ed, which shirt would you wear if you were me?"

"The blue one," he answered.

"The blue one it is," I said.

There was a giant quilt of excitement draped across our apartment, smothering all my anticipated jitters. Even Ed seemed like an all right guy.

"Tonight's the big night, Ed," I announced. "I'm going to ask Bronwyn to marry me."

The corners of Ed's mouth brushed up against his ears as he executed one of the biggest smiles I had ever seen.

"That's fantastic," he said. "Can you keep a secret?" he asked.

"Can I tell Bronwyn?"

"Oh, sure, that's a gimme."

"Then I can keep a secret," I replied.

"Tonight's the night for Sharon and me as well."

"No," I said, bothered by the coincidence.

With both our secrets out in the open, our apartment became some sort of weird cubicle of hope and possibility. "Isn't this great?" Ed kept saying as he unloaded and loaded the dishwasher. He began bouncing off the walls about twenty minutes before it was time for him to leave. Twice I thought he was having some sort of convulsion and that I should call the paramedics. But it was nothing, just Ed dealing the best he could with preproposal jitters. He hugged me as he left—he was in love. He even forgot to spray his hair with Rogaine. He had obviously gone from smitten to bitten.

The telephone rang just as I was getting out of the shower. I drenched the carpet running to answer it. It was my dad. I was amazed. Had my dad been so in tune with me as to know that this was the big day?

"Ian," my dad's voice was wavering.

"Dad, is everything okay?"

"I'm fine, Son. It's just that, well, I was arrested last night. They still think I was involved in some way with the information theft."

What was going on? This was the call the wayward son was supposed to make to the frustrated father. "Dad, I crashed your new car into the old McDonald's, and now I'm in jail. I'm sorry, I'll never do it again, please forgive me."

"I'm home now, and there is not much more they can do to me. I didn't do it. You know that don't you?"

"Of course, Dad. Can I help at all?"

This whole thing was ridiculous, my father, suspected of and arrested for stealing. The man who insisted we pay tithing on the estimated worth of all our Christmas presents was being accused of being on the take.

"Thanks, but I think we've got it all under control at the moment. I just wanted you to know what happened before you heard it from some other source."

We talked for a few more minutes and then hung up. I changed my shirt and left my father and the worry of what was happening in the hamper next to the blue shirt Ed preferred. I had other things to think of now.

The afternoon sky was gray, broken up here and there by the furry hands of green leaves. We were to meet at the big tree outside Bronwyn's apartments.

The top of the tree came into view; then she was there, leaning against the tree, her blue eyes searching for me. Her hair was loose and blowing all over. The dark bark of the tree behind her made her white teeth glow, and the black centers of her eyes made my shoulders throb. It was a wonderful feeling.

She took my hand and pulled me toward her. I suddenly wished every person I ever knew could be here to witness this beautiful girl and her acceptance of me.

Though no definites had been discussed, we both seemed to sense the importance of this particular date. We walked arm-in-arm down the street—her on the edge of the curb and me in the gutter, making her a little closer to my height. It was nice spacing.

It wasn't long before we reached the massive, temporary chain-link fence that, for the next couple of weeks, would surround the carnival. Cheap, loud, calliope music filled the air. We got in line to buy ride tickets.

"What should we go on first?" I asked.

She looked around, taking everything in with one glance.

"Carnivals are all the same," she said. "The only thing I ever trust is the Ferris wheel."

I had been afraid she would say that.

"I don't do so well on Ferris wheels," I admitted.

She sensed a weak spot.

"You're not scared are you?"

I decided to be honest with her. After all, a few hours from now she was quite possibly going to be my fiancée.

"No."

"Then let's do it," she smiled.

I really was not a big fan of the Ferris wheel. Years before, when my family had been visiting an uncle back East, the Ferris wheel at their state fair had completely tipped over. According to the news report the carnival workers had failed to secure it properly, and a strong wind toppled it. No one had been on it at the time, but when it fell over it wiped out two other rides, a snow cone shack, every prize-winning goat, and the runner-up pigs. The grisly scene had left a mighty impression on me. Now, flashes of those images sprang through my head as I forced myself toward that big wheel with swaying seats. This would be the first time since the accident that I dared to ride the wheel.

"Tickets, please," the ride attendant said.

We gave him our tickets and walked forward. I was trapped. I should have been honest. I should have just told Bronwyn that I was a really big chicken when it came to

Ferris wheels. And could she please wait until some other time to scar me for life.

We seated ourselves in the swaying seat and clamped the safety bar tightly into place. The sound it made as it snapped shut was horrifying. A light wind picked up as the ride jolted into motion. I thought about jumping while we were still low enough, but Bronwyn slipped her hand into mine, and I momentarily forgot my fears.

I'm not a coward. I could ride the Zippy Twirl upside down for hours and never even twitch. But I was young when I saw that other wheel tumble—young and impressionable. Now, like varicose veins, my fears were slowly rising to the surface. I took a few deep breaths as the wheel speed increased to just below that of light. The wind ran through our hair and around our bodies, forcing us to move closer to each other for warmth. Bronwyn's presence was like healing balm applied to a dead carcass—nice thought, but ultimately ineffective.

"I wish this ride would never end," Bronwyn shouted.

What a waste of a wish, I thought. Now if we had been sitting together on the miniature train, chugging lazily around the park, I think I would have agreed. But we were locked into a heavy metal seat that was attached to some spokes by a few stripped screws and rusted bolts. And we were going nowhere fast.

Just as I was beginning to give up all hope, the ride started to slow down. I was feeling as if I had just conquered a major Goliath, when they stopped the ride at the seat right in front of us. It was clear that we would now be the last ones to get off. Cart by cart we moved up until we were stopped at the very top.

The minutes ticked on, and still we hadn't moved. Bronwyn began lightly rocking our chair. I didn't want to sound overanxious or panicked, so as coolly as I could I insisted, "Stop it!"

"Hey," she paused. "There's a bunch of people standing around down there. And they're pointing at us."

I didn't want to look

"It looks like they're yelling something."

"What are they saying?" I asked.

"I don't know, they're too far away."

I decided to look for myself. I tested the safety bar to see if it was still locked and then leaned my head over and peered at the people down below. They were definitely looking at us. I sat back and exhaled.

"What do you think they're doing?" I asked.

"I don't know, something must be broken."

"Broken?"

"I'm sure they'll have it fixed in—"

She stopped mid-sentence, her eyes fixed on something.

"What is it?" I asked loudly.

"There's a man climbing up toward us; it's amazing, he looks like a monkey."

I didn't want to look over the rail again.

"What kind of man?" I asked. "I mean, does he look like a worker, or some sort of maniac that feeds on broken Ferris wheel prey?"

"I don't know," she said. "He looks to be somewhere in between the two."

She sat back and moved in close to me. I put both my arms around her and prepared to protect her from this approaching menace. We could hear him saying something to the people in the cart down and in front of us. Then a head covered with greasy brown hair emerged from beneath us. The next thing we knew a strange man was kneeling on the edge of our chair, cracking his knuckles. It was clear that Bronwyn's parents had never given her the "Stranger Danger" talk because she instantly began a conversation with this man.

"That's amazing. How did you climb that?"

"Oh, it's nothing," he said. "Once when the Whirl Barrel ride got jammed I had to climb all the way up to the top of it and run on it like those loggers that run on logs in the cartoons."

"Pretty incredible," Bronwyn said.

The guy's chest swelled as he knelt there beaming with pride. I was tired of not knowing.

"Do you know what the problem is?" I asked.

"Problem?" he eyed me.

"With the Ferris wheel," I clarified.

"Oh," he said, "the whole gear thing broke out. It's really messed up." He held his hands up and opened and closed them in front of his face as if that would describe the problem.

"How long will we be up here?" I wanted answers.

"Well, unless you want to climb down, it could be quite a while."

"We can't climb down," I said, sounding more afraid than I had wanted to. "I mean, can't you see we have a girl here?"

"Sure I see there is a girl here," he said with raised eyebrows. "But that don't matter none. It's still going to take a long time to fix."

"What about the fire department?" I asked. "Don't they

have a really long ladder or something?" My true colors were beginning to show, and I'm pretty sure that at that moment, both Bronwyn and this monkey guy saw an awful lot of yellow.

"The fire department does have some pretty dang long ladders, it's just that . . . oh, by the way, my name's Don Gull." He stuck his hand out and shook both of ours. "You see, none of their ladders would even come close to being long enough. They do have this really cool lift thing that they are sending over. It should come up to about three feet below the cart down and in front of you. The people in that seat are willing to jump three feet, but it don't come anywhere near your cart. You could climb down about twenty feet and then get onto the lift. But let me advise you that climbing this thing isn't as easy as it looks."

"I'm sure it isn't; we'll wait here," Bronwyn said.

Like we had a choice.

"Suit yourselves," Don said. "It's awful pretty tonight. Of course, I like it when it rains."

And with that he was gone.

We looked at each other and smiled.

"Well, here we are," Bronwyn said, "alone at last. Are you going to be all right?"

"Sure, this has all the makings of a perfect night. The possibility of rain, literally trapped and suspended a hundred feet above the earth, and alone with the girl of my dreams. Perfect."

I really was somewhat okay with the situation. It's just that I had a certain role to play, and I planned to play it well.

"So, what should we do?" I asked, half-smiling.

"Well, you have a captive audience, anything you would like to ask me?" Bronwyn smiled a knowing smile.

"Yeah, as a matter of fact there is. Do you remember years ago when your family invited our family over to your house for dinner?"

"Yes."

"Do you remember how your mom kept calling me pudgy?"

"I'm sorry, she has a knack for making people feel little," Bronwyn smirked.

"You mean big. Anyhow, my real question is, were you in love with me then, or was that just my overly hopeful imagination?"

She looked at me, cheeks pink from the cold and blue eyes smiling. "That's your question?"

I nodded yes.

"I can remember that my mom served a turkey stuffed with corn bread stuffing and surrounded by cooked carrots that I had peeled. My dad wore his blue and yellow striped shirt; your mom wore a bright red dress and kept apologizing for being overdressed. You asked for the potatoes to be passed to you three times before anyone heard, and I asked to be excused early but was denied the request. I can remember all of that, and very clearly. I just can't remember if I was madly in love with you or not. Oh, well, if by some chance I was, I'm sure most of it's faded by now." She held her hand out to test the sky for rain. "So, do you have any real questions to ask me?" Bronwyn teased.

"Nope, that's all I care to know. Ignorance is bliss," I said.

"No wonder you're always so happy," Bronwyn replied. "Can I ask you a question now?"

"Turnabout's fair play," I consented.

"What's your middle name?"

My middle name? What kind of question was that? Some things were meant to be left alone. Some questions should never be asked. I had no desire for her to know my middle name. I could lie. I could tell her something really common and unimpressive. Then the question could be put quietly to rest. But there was a lot more at stake here. Did I want to start out our eternity together honestly, or on a note of falsehood? What if I lied to her and years from now as she was trying to do our genealogy she stumbled upon the truth, what then? Would it pop up to drive a giant wedge into our then well-seasoned relationship? I could change our family records, but that would be tampering with history. I thought carefully. She knew my middle name began with "J"—it was burnt into my scripture cover. So, even if I lied, my choices would be limited. I decided to start out our eternity on a note of falsehood. I'd tell her the truth later after she had said I do.

"Joseph."

"Oh, really?" she said. "So if you went by your middle name instead of Ian, you'd be Joseph Smith."

"Well, of course I wouldn't be the real Joseph Smith."

"Of course," she said.

She seemed to believe me. She was even saying my full name aloud to see how it sounded.

"I like it," she said. "It's a very impressive name."

"I'm glad you approve." I tried to change the subject. "It's sure taking a long time to fix this thing."

Bronwyn, however, insisted on beating this middle name thing into the ground.

"So, where does your Aunt Joseph live?" she asked.

"My Aunt Joseph?"

"Yeah, your sister Kate said you had the same middle name as one of your aunts."

I had been caught.

"But since she said you had the same name as your Aunt Jan, she must not know your Aunt Joseph."

It was too late for the truth. "Continue the lie," my brain whispered. So, like a good body, I obeyed my head.

"Sure, Kate knows Aunt Joseph. It's just that we always called her Aunt Jan because of her profession." I was getting in too deep.

"What's her profession?" Bronwyn asked.

It was all I could think of. "She's a janitor."

Luckily a fireman began speaking to us through a bull-horn from the chair right below.

"Are you two still doing okay?"

"We'll be much better when we're back on the ground," I hollered back.

"I can imagine," he said.

"How much longer until it's fixed?" Bronwyn asked.

What was the matter? Wasn't she having a good time? How much longer until it's fixed? That's the kind of question I was supposed to ask, not her.

"It looks like it will be a few more hours."

"It's getting dark," I yelled. "Couldn't you just find or build a bigger ladder?"

I could see the fireman's head shake. We watched as he lowered himself down, eventually becoming a toy man surrounded by other toy people.

"Not quite the night you had planned?" Bronwyn asked.

178

"No, this is exactly what I had planned. Except it was supposed to be the Whirl Barrel ride that we got stuck on. That way, Don could have run romantically above us, like in the cartoons."

"Oh, that would have been nice," she hummed.

It was beginning to rain harder, and the cold breeze was making our bodies a breeding ground for goose bumps and shivers. I gave Bronwyn my jacket in an attempt to be chivalrous. I was sort of hoping she would reject the offer, but she gladly accepted it. We played a rousing game of paper, scissors, rock. That kept our minds occupied for about three minutes. When Bronwyn just kept doing rock, I knew her heart was no longer really in the game. The sky blackened, giving us a chance to search for the first star in an attempt to wish upon it. Unfortunately, the heavens were too stuffed with rain clouds to show any stars. So our search was futile from the start.

"My father was arrested last night." It was blunt, but I could think of no other way to say it.

"Arrested?"

"He's not in jail. I guess he's out on bail. Weird, huh? My father out on bail."

"I hate the whole situation," Bronwyn said. "Why don't they just arrest Brian and lock him up regardless of whether he actually did it or not?"

"Sounds good to me," I said, warming at the thought of it. The people working on the Ferris wheel dropped something large and metal. It clanged loudly against the ground when it hit. My faith in our Ferris wheel saviors was dwindling.

"So, have you made up your mind yet about going to school this summer?" Bronwyn asked.

"I'm not going," I said, spitting out the rain that had fallen on my lips. "I need to finish some projects at my house. I've only got a few more little things to do before it's completely done." The pride I felt for my soon-to-be-accomplished accomplishment was evident.

"Do you remember years ago in Sunday School class," Bronwyn asked, "right after the old house your parents bought you burned down? And you kept bringing it up in class? You were kind of bragging about the fact that you owned a burnt field. But then Jack Brewer told you to shut up about your stupid field."

I nodded. Rain from the top of my head flowed down over my eyes.

"I remember being completely jealous of you and that dumb plot of land."

"You can borrow it sometime," I offered.

She smiled and leaned against me. We sat in silence for a while, letting the rain do all the talking as it plinked against our cold skin.

It had been about an hour since we had had any sort of communication with others. Bronwyn had talked me into opening the safety rail so that we could actually move and be more comfortable—it did nothing to comfort me. The jacket I had lent her was now soaked through.

"I think I would be warmer without this," she said, peeling the jacket off.

I nodded, not really focusing on what she was saying. I was more interested in the jacket itself. It was nothing great, just my green flannel one with a thrice-broken zipper. But for some reason, as she took it off and fiddled around with it, my mind wanted me to pay attention. Bronwyn shook the jacket in an attempt to get some to the water out of it.

"Where should I put this?" she said, not wanting to lay the wet thing on either of us and holding only a corner of it.

I sat there unable to say anything as my mind slowly helped me remember why the jacket was of such worth. In the small, inside pocket with the half-cracked button was a box. A box with a ring in it. A ring with a hope attached to it. A hope which appeared to be on the verge of being dashed.

I leaped out of my seat to grab the jacket as I watched the wind twist and tease it out of Bronwyn's hand. Catching the coat was surprisingly easy. The problem now was that I had jumped out of my seat. My attempt to save a ring that I would have been paying off for the next three years was hurling me to my death. Images of Bronwyn and me exchanging vows made it hard for me to focus in on the open safety bar. It was either grab onto it, or plunge a hundred feet to an early death.

I grabbed it with my right hand. I shoved the sleeve of the jacket into my mouth and bit down hard so I could put my left hand on the safety bar. The plunge was temporarily postponed. I could hear Bronwyn yelling something, and a gasp was rising from the distant crowd below, tickling my stomach and causing my grip to weaken. My right heel was caught on the lip of our chair, saving me from having to rely on just my arms to keep me supported. The chair was rocking wildly. I closed my eyes and prayed. The words were confused and the structure poor, but the plea was earnest: "Please don't let me fall!"

Bronwyn had both hands on my ankle and was trying to

pull me in. It wasn't working. I thought about just letting go and hopefully landing on something soft, but from this height, even something soft would kill me. Bronwyn let go of my leg and grabbed on to the safety bar where it was hinged to our seat. She began to pull. It was working. I lifted my other foot back into the cart, and soon my behind was back on the seat with the safety bar locked securely into place. Bronwyn threw her arms around me.

"I hate Ferris wheels," I was finally able to mutter.

"I love you," she said.

A bunch of words followed that, but I couldn't tell you what they were. All I can remember is "I love you" and the tone of voice she used. I wasn't someone she was casually dating or a pit stop on the way to celestial bliss. She really loved me. We could see an ambulance and a couple of news vans racing toward the park.

"Tell me they're not here for us," I groaned.

"I think they are," Bronwyn answered, still shaken up from me almost falling.

The night was now officially dark, and we were definitely wet. I'd heard humans are made up of 73 percent water, but at the moment we had pushed our percentage to 99.9. With the rain coming down as hard as it was we found it necessary to sit as close to each other as possible. I tried hard not to talk much because each time I did my teeth would chatter uncontrollably. Bronwyn was having the same problem, except on her it was cute. Once again we could see the fire platform being lifted toward us. There were three people on it, and it lifted slowly due to their weight. I recognized the fireman from before. Next to him was a man with a TV camera, and next to that man was a local news reporter whom I recognized.

"Smile," Bronwyn whispered.

I frowned.

"Hey, you two, try and catch these," the fireman yelled.

He threw something orange and square at us; he missed. He tried again with another. It hit me in the face and then fell into my arms. The next one I caught perfectly. They were just plain orange ponchos, yet we opened them like we were six-year-olds opening our biggest presents on Christmas morning. Bronwyn's went on easily. Mine, however, had a right sleeve that was sewn shut at the shoulder. I looked over at Bronwyn, her orange poncho aglow from the Ferris wheel lights. Rain was splashing and running down her as she smiled at me.

Something moved me.

"Bronwyn?" I asked.

"Yes," she replied.

Something moved me back.

"Nothing," I brushed it off.

"Hey, kids," the reporter yelled. "We'll be putting you on the ten o'clock news. Do you have anything that you would like to say?" he hollered.

Bronwyn spoke up. "He was just about to ask me to marry him," she yelled nicely. "Could we have a few minutes alone?"

Was I that easy to read? And more importantly, did that mean she was prepared to say yes? I pushed my left eyebrow up with my right hand. My face was cold and wet, but my body was burning, sending light impulses down my arms and legs and shooting them out my toes and fingers. The fire lift lowered a bit, but I could see they were still filming. The world was waiting, and soon my name would be known for good and evil among all of Channel Four's viewers. The pressure was great. I reached into my jacket pocket for the ring. Bronwyn smiled as she realized the reason I had gone to such lengths to save my coat.

"Bronwyn?" I managed to get out. I tried as hard as possible to get myself into some sort of kneeling position. "I was wondering," I continued. "Well, this isn't exactly where or how I planned to ask, but, Bronwyn, will you marry me?"

"Of course."

I hugged her with my one free arm, feeling happier than a person should feel. My heart was bouncing around inside of me, making me jumpy and pleasantly unsettled. The Ferris wheel joined in by jerking into motion. Just when things were getting good, we were heading down. We reached the bottom in no time. Bronwyn held her ring up to the crowd, and they responded with a giant roar of approval. I felt as if I should give a speech. But even if I had been that kind of person—one who gives speeches, that is—my legs were too numb to allow me stand. So we just sat there in our bright, safety-orange ponchos on the Ferris wheel chair that we had come to know so well, answering questions about being trapped, my brush with death, and our happy ending. We were both glad when my legs were working again and we were able to flee the scene.

After we changed into dry clothes, we spent the rest of the night sitting together on Bronwyn's couch watching all the different accounts of what they were now calling the "Ferris Wheel of Fate" incident. I got a little sick of seeing the clip of the poncho hitting me in the face. And only one channel got my name right. But I enjoyed Bronwyn resting her head on my shoulder, testing out her soon-to-be new name.

It was midnight as I walked myself home. The rain had stopped, leaving the air extremely clean, and the streetlights shining lazily upon the moist lawns and soggy streets. A long way off, a dog barked, starting a chain reaction that ended with the small beagle that was locked in the house I was now passing.

Our apartment was lit up and waiting for me when I arrived. Ed was leaning back in one of the kitchen chairs reading some blue book. He smiled, showing me all his teeth and most of his gums.

"How was your night?" he asked, closing his book, sitting up straight, and crossing his legs.

"Fine," I answered. Ed was acting unusually cool, and I could sense that more than just about anything, he wanted me to ask him about Sharon. I decided to make him suffer.

"So, Ed, what are you reading?" I asked.

It was not the question he wanted, his countenance frowned. He looked at the cover of his book to remember the title.

"Oh, it's just a book of American love poems." He couldn't take it any longer. "Sharon said, yes. Can you believe it? Looks like we will be getting married after I graduate. And I was wondering . . ."

Oh, please, no.

"I was wondering if you will be my best man?"

Obviously the Ferris wheel incident hadn't taught me enough humility. The gods were picking on me tonight. As much as I wanted to say no, my reply was just the opposite.

"Sure, I'd be honored to."

185

"Great. I knew you would do it." He picked up the phone and dialed Sharon. His side of the conversation went like this:

"Hi. Yes! No. Really? Three. You bet! (small forced laugh) I love you. Bye." He hung the phone up. "She says thanks."

"You're both welcome," I said. "I'm going to bed. I'll see you in the morning."

"Hey, wait a minute. Did you ask Bronwyn?"

"Yes."

"Well, what did she say?" Ed asked.

"Yes."

Ed's congratulations fell on deaf ears. I was already down the hall, in my room, and asleep before my head hit the pillow. Half an hour later Ed woke me up.

"Why didn't you tell me?" He asked as he shook me.

"Tell you what, Ed? Just go away and let me sleep," I mumbled.

"About the carnival, and getting stuck, and almost dying." In my half-conscious state, Ed sounded on the verge of tears.

"I'll tell you in the morning, now let me get some sleep." I buried my head deep in my pillow, knowing full well that Ed wouldn't give up that easy.

"In the morning?" he huffed. "I had no idea that you were so selfish. What about me? How do you think this makes me feel? My best friend almost dies, and I am the last to know." Ed was pacing the room now. "What about my wedding? What about you being my best man? Don't you think that I should be made aware of things like this? I would have had to change my plans and find a new best man." I kept wishing he was closer to me so that I could hit him without having to get up. He continued, "No man is an island you know. Are

186

you listening to me, Ian? Let me in, let me be a part of your life, like I'm letting you be a part of mine."

"Go out, Ed. I'll talk about this tomorrow."

He was just getting started.

"When I think of you just walking in here tonight and going straight to bed without mentioning a thing. Well, it makes me so mad. It causes me to think things that would keep me from getting to the celestial kingdom."

"I'm sure God will forgive you."

"Okay, Mister Insensitive, go ahead and get your precious sleep. If your conscience will let you, that is. We'll continue this conversation in the morning. That is, if I'm still talking to you."

A person can dream.

He slammed the door as he left the room, leaving me to have one of the soundest sleeps I had ever experienced.

21

THE MORNING AFTER

The early morning sunlight pricked me with its warmth as a large gathering of birds argued outside my window. I was depressed for some reason. My whole body refused to move, and gravity was pushing me deep into my mattress. I could hear Ed moving about in the TV room. Knowing that I would have to have a lengthy conversation with him before I could ever get out of the apartment depressed me even more. Just where did he get the idea that he and I were best friends? Certainly there were others who tolerated him as much as I did. I was in a true-to-life bad mood, something that did not happen to me often. I had no reason to be grumpy. Last night, despite a few unplanned mishaps, had turned out all right. I was engaged. Sure, I was going to have to be Ed's best man. But worst-case scenario, I might have to stand around staring at Ed in a white tux for a few hours. Ed knocked on the door.

"What?" I snapped.

"Just wondering if you would like to catch an early matinee with me," he almost sang.

What was it with him? Did he think that last night's

coincidence of both of us asking our girlfriends to be our wives instantly transformed us into bosom buddies? Why would I want to go to the movies with a guy who bragged about how many times he had seen *The Little Mermaid?* I could think of nothing more detrimental to my mental well-being than spending the day at the movies with Ed. Besides, wasn't he supposed to be mad at me for not telling him all about my night?

"No thanks," I yelled back.

"Well, excuse me," he pouted. I could hear him stomping away from the door. I felt smug and good about refusing his offer. Maybe if I treated him badly he'd even withdraw his best man invitation. I had better things to do than stand around at some reception so he could prove to people that he had friends. I was engaged to Bronwyn. The most beautiful girl on the entire campus had willingly given her consent to spend the rest of her eternity with me. Certainly that made me better than the average Ed.

I couldn't believe I was thinking these things. The truly frightening part was that I was enjoying it. Things looked differently now; perhaps I had been living life the wrong way. The joy of being better than others was an uncharted area for me, and the temptation to explore it was very strong this morning. I slid out of bed and into some comfortable clothes. Maybe my problem was that I had been catering to humility instead of making it my victim. I needed to turn the tables. I had been eating off the plate of meekness—it was time for new dinnerware.

I walked out into the kitchen. Ed was sitting at the table adding some figures. I opened the cupboard and took out my box of cereal. The box was empty. My newfound personality boiled.

"Did you eat this?" I continued without waiting for an answer. "You eat all my cereal and then put the empty box back?" I sounded like someone I would hate, but I continued. "Do not eat my cereal. Do you understand?"

Ed's face reddened, from ear to ear and from his weak chin to his balding head.

I had more to say. "Just because it so happens that we both got engaged last night doesn't give you permission to jump out of bed this morning and eat my food." I wasn't yelling or screaming, but I was being a jerk.

"I'm sorry," Ed said, embarrassed for both of us.

"I'm sorry doesn't always cut—" I most likely would have gone on for hours if it hadn't been for the bolt of lightning sent from heaven. It came in the form of me tripping on the edge of the carpet. I fell face first onto the tile kitchen floor. It happened so fast that I had no time to absorb the impact with my hands or twist to avoid hitting my face. I landed nose first. A giant pop echoed loudly throughout the apartment, and blood, like fireworks, began squirting out of my nose. I rolled off of my face and onto my forehead. It shook my brain and made it hard for me to focus on anything. I could make out Ed running back and forth, finally stopping right in front of me. He shoved a wet, checkered washcloth into my face, hoping to stop the blood. He kept asking me if I was all right, but I couldn't get my brain to tell my mouth to mumble yes.

I heard the doorbell ring and within a couple seconds Ed had answered it and was back in the kitchen with Sharon and three of her friends.

"He just tripped and fell on his face," I heard Ed say. "I think his nose is broken."

190

Someone asked Ed if I should be taken to the hospital.

"If the bleeding doesn't stop soon," he answered.

My vision had cleared up so that I could now see everyone. They all had grim expressions on their faces, staring at me as if I were the victim of some facial surgery gone horribly wrong.

Ed rolled up his sleeve, "You've got to keep pressure on that," he said. He kneeled down next to me. "Sharon, wet another towel for him, will you?" Ed took the bloody towel off my nose and looked things over, then put the clean one on. "I think you'll be all right; do you remember your name?" he asked.

"I know my name."

He turned to the crowd of four.

"He remembers his name. He's going to be all right."

Ed went to the sink and began to rinse out the checkered washcloth. He twisted it to get as much water out as possible and then draped it softly over the spigot. I saw his eyes connect with Sharon's. The lighting in the kitchen wasn't the best, but it was easy to see that Sharon was glowing with pride. Her Ed had the situation under control and was handling the crisis sensibly.

I sort of smiled. "Ed, I'm sorry about what I was saying, I—"

"Don't worry about it," he insisted.

Sharon slid her arm through Ed's. "It doesn't look too bad," she said politely.

I left them in the kitchen to clean up the blood so that I could see my nose firsthand. I wish the mirror could have lied just a bit—my nose was swollen and already discolored. I looked awful.

Bronwyn called, and we agreed to meet at the cafeteria in two hours. I didn't tell her about my nose. I figured if I was there to talk her through her reaction, she might still like me in the end. I took a shower and was enjoying my second bowl of Shredded Wheat (as much as you can enjoy eating Shredded Wheat with a plug of bloody tissue in both nostrils) when my home teachers arrived. It was a surprise visit. They had seen me on the news last night and were curious to know more.

"What happened to your nose?" the tall blond one named Roger asked.

"Well, I—"

Russ, the other one, interrupted. "Didn't you see him get hit in the face with that poncho?"

"A poncho did that?" Roger asked in amazement. "The damage looks more extensive than—"

"Well, actually—" I tried to jump in.

Russ interrupted my interruption. "Those ponchos are pretty hard when they're still packaged. When we took the Scouts on the last campout, we used two of them to steady that wobbly table, remember?" he asked Roger.

"Oh, at Lake Spirit Wand? Yes, I remember," Roger said.

I thought about just going back to the kitchen and letting them continue their conversation, but that would have been rude.

"Not Lake Spirit Wand," Russ whined. "We didn't even take ponchos to Lake Spirit Wand. I'm talking about Hidden Pond."

"Now, Russ, you know as well as I do that I didn't even go on the outing to Hidden Pond. I was helping the Scouts with their merit badge roundup."

"Brother Morley."

192

"Brother Toone," he countered.

"Listen, guys, I would love to keep talking, but I've got to meet my fiancée in less than an hour."

"Gonna tie the old knot, huh?" Roger asked.

"Yes, it looks like it." I was trying as hard as I could to shoo them toward the door.

"Not me," Russ chimed in. "It would take one special lady to get me to give up the bachelor life."

"Amen to that," Roger said.

"Don't you guys have some camping thing to attend or something?" I asked.

"They are showing that safety movie at the sports store," Roger remembered. "We'd better go, Ian."

"I understand."

Russ took my hand and shook it earnestly. "Sorry to run, but we just wanted to see how things are with you. Looks like everything's all right. Let us know if we can help in any way, okay?"

"I sure will, thanks," I said.

Roger handed me a business card that read: "In case of emergency, call your home teachers." It was the fifth one they had given me. Roger informed me that he had sprayed the card with flame retardant just in case the emergency happened to be fire.

"How thoughtful," I said as I closed the door on them.

They stood outside my apartment talking to each other for at least five more minutes before they finally got into their car and drove off.

I raced to get ready to meet Bronwyn. I was late before I even left.

22
WHEN PUSH COMES TO LOVE

On my way to the cafeteria I ran into Brenda, a girl who had been bugging me to take her out for quite some time. I joyfully told her that I was already engaged and that it would now be impossible for us to ever go out. I thought she took it a little too well.

Bronwyn was sitting in a booth at the cafeteria waiting for me. She was talking to some guy with really big hands and a small nose. I had no need to be jealous. She had pledged herself to me.

Neither of them looked up or responded to me standing there.

I cleared my throat as politely as I could.

Bronwyn smiled, stared at my nose, patted the seat next to her, and then continued to talk to this guy.

I sat down.

"What's going on?" I asked nicely, acting as if her ignoring me didn't bother me in the least.

"I'll tell you later," she said to me. "Thanks," she said to this other guy. He jumped up and jogged off.

"Who was that?" I asked.

"He's one of my brother's old mission companions."

"He didn't look too old," I said, risking sounding a little jealous.

"What happened to your face?" she asked. I think she was concerned.

"I tripped."

"I thought people stopped tripping after the age of ten," Bronwyn laughed.

"Most people do."

"Guess what happened last night?" she asked, no longer smiling.

"We got engaged."

"Besides that," she said.

"Could anything else matter?" I asked.

"Unfortunately, this does," she sighed. "My dad was arrested."

I knew it, I thought to myself. Almost falling from the top of a Ferris wheel and dying was getting off too easy.

"We're engaged," I said as if that was the answer to this problem.

"I know, but I'm going to go back home to help my mother for awhile."

"You can't leave now," I reasoned. "Finals are in a month."

It all made sense now, she had just said yes to me because she knew something like this was going to happen. This was all part of her plan.

"It will be all right," she tried to smile.

"So how long's awhile?"

"I'm not sure."

"What about our engagement?"

"We'll just be apart for a bit, that's all. This will soon smooth out, and then we can get married." She picked up a nacho chip, now soggy from her lack of attention, grimaced at it, then set it back down.

Why didn't she lean over and kiss me? Why didn't she move in closer to me and tell me how much she loved me and that no matter what, we were going to be together? Why didn't she soothe my worried brow with her warm hands? The fact of the matter was she didn't even offer me a mushy nacho, much less do any of the above. Here I was, on what was supposed to be a day filled with a glorious afterglow from the previous night, while in reality it radiated with the smell of garbage left out years before.

"I've got to go find a way to get out of all my classes. Do you want to come?" she asked.

"How are you getting back home to Sterling?"

"John Prestwich is going to take me."

"John?" I asked.

"My brother's old companion. He's heading through Sterling on his way to pick up his sister."

How convenient, I thought.

We spent the rest of the day together getting things ready and telling each other how much we were going to miss one another. We thought about really cementing our relationship by getting one of those old-time western photos taken of the two of us. But with my nose swollen like it was, decided against it. Besides, I had never looked good in a vest.

I got up at five the next morning to see her and John off. I had spent a good fifteen minutes splashing cold water on my puffy, early morning eyes, but I still ended up looking sub-par and half awake.

"So you'll come down next weekend?" Bronwyn asked as we said our good-byes.

"Of course."

John honked for the third time.

"I love you," she whispered.

"I know," I bragged. Her lips moved toward mine, and with a kiss she was out the door and into the car. I waved at her, but I couldn't see her wave back due to her luggage being crammed up in the back window of John's car.

I went back to my room and crawled back in bed just as Ed got up for his early morning exercises.

23

(S)PAIN

I was sort of (and I mean sort of in the most uncommitted way), getting back into the swing of things. Bronwyn was hours away, but we had plenty of phone conversations, and for the first time in my life, absence was making my heart grow fonder. Her dad had a much rougher time with the police than my father had. Because Mr. Innaway was now out of work, he and his wife had sold their home and were living in an apartment. Of course, unlike my family, where everyone just hung around until my parents lost all sanity, Brother and Sister Innaway had successfully reared and gotten rid of all their children—some of them even lived hundreds of miles away. So, now only Bronwyn was with them, and I knew from experience that she was absolutely no trouble at all.

I even made breakfast for Ed one morning. Nothing elaborate. I just dumped some cereal into a slightly dirty bowl and poured some milk over it. He was moved beyond words. Things were going all right.

Then my father called and told me that he, too, needed to sell our house.

"Do you think we could move into your place? Just until this whole mess is cleared up?" he asked me. It had not been easy for my dad to ask, but it was surprisingly easy for me to answer.

"Sure, Dad."

I heard a noise like the rushing of the Holy Ghost through the streets of Kirtland during the temple dedication—my father's sigh of relief. I couldn't believe he could have thought I was capable of saying no.

"I know it's your place, but it would really help us out."

"Dad, it's no problem. Honest."

I wanted to be sentimental. This was a story to send to the *Ensign*. Son willingly repays his father a small portion of what he has been given. The son would be a person of great humility and the analogy grand. But the only thing I could actually think was, What have I done? It's one thing to pay back my father and mother, but my brother and sister? It's so much easier to be charitable when you know that those you are being charitable to appreciate it. Without so much as a grain of thanks, my brother and sister would tread the carpet I had installed and slam the cabinets I had put up.

I tried writing Bronwyn once, thinking it would be a romantic gesture. But the words my pen poured out were poor-looking and uninspired.

"What are you writing?"

"I'm trying to write a letter, Ed."

"To whom?" he asked, making proper English sound incredibly stupid.

"Bronwyn."

199

"But you just talked to her on the phone last night, and you most likely will talk to her again tonight. What could you possibly say in a letter that wouldn't be old news by the time she received it?"

I crumbled up the paper and leaned back in my chair.

"You going out with Sharon tonight?"

"Need you ask?"

I really didn't need to. Ed and Sharon were inseparable; every night was date night with them. And as usual, I was glad that he would be out of the apartment so that I could talk to Bronwyn privately without him picking up the phone every five minutes and asking if we were still talking. Someone knocked on our door.

"That would be my future wife," Ed said, jumping up and clicking his heels as he ran to the door. I sneaked as quickly as I could to the sanctity of my room, where I lay on my bed with the light off and tried to think of an original thought so that my brain would have something to do. There was a soft knock on the door.

"Who is it?"

The door opened slowly.

"Are you dressed?" Ed asked.

"Yes."

The door opened the rest of the way. Someone was there, but it wasn't Ed, it was Bronwyn. Like the pillar of fire that had led Moses, she lit up the room and drew me up and over. My chin knocked her forehead as we kissed.

Ed spoke up. "I thought it was Sharon, but it was Bronwyn. I was as shocked as you are."

Couldn't Ed see that we were too engrossed in each other

to accurately hear what he was saying? Someone else knocked on the front door, and Ed went to answer it.

"Why are you here?" I asked Bronwyn.

"I didn't know I needed a reason to come."

"You don't, I'm just really glad that you did."

I kissed her, she kissed me, we kissed each other. Then we walked out into the living room and sat down with Sharon, who had just come in.

"Where's Ed?" I asked Sharon.

"He's spraying his hair," she replied.

Ed came out of the bathroom, his hair sparkling as if the dews of heaven had distilled upon him. He helped Sharon up and then the two of them left to do whatever it was they did.

Bronwyn and I were alone. She was right here, right now, and that was all that mattered for the moment. We had taken care of all the small talk during our phone conversations, so she just started right in on the reason she had come.

"I want to know what you think about something. I've sort of made a decision, and I want to run it past you."

"What kind of decision?" I asked.

"Well, living with my parents isn't very easy. My dad is so stressed out that every time I look at him I want to cry, and I know that it's going to be at least a couple months until this is actually over. And, well, I can't come back to school; I mean, I've missed too much to recover." She took a deep breath. "So what would you think if I spent a month in Spain with my aunt? It would only be a short while and I could sort some things out and try to find myself in all this mess. My aunt has a free ticket for me, thanks to her frequent-flyer points."

201

"Spain?" I asked in disbelief. "The one across the ocean?"

"You're not letting me finish," she said, filling her lungs with air. "When I get back we can get married. Things will be less hectic and less confused. It would only be for a short while. It might be just what we need. And it will give us some time to do this thing right. Plus, it might be my one chance in life to go to Spain." Bronwyn exhaled. "What do you think?"

I wanted to be upset. I wanted to strut around and tell her how it was going to be. I wanted to go on and on about the way a patriarchal society ran. I wanted to say, You'll stay right here, missy, and do as I wish. But she was smarter than me, which meant her decision was probably the right one. She also had that womanly gift, the gift of deciding things with her heart and mind, and not just her feelings. I was beaten. The only thing for me to do now was to act like I had had this idea before her.

"I've been having some similar thoughts."

"You have?" she asked, surprised.

"No, I haven't," I broke down. "Don't you have any family that live a bit closer? What about that uncle of yours who lives just down the street from my parents? The poor guy spends his days completely alone. You could stay with him and help him."

"That's not my uncle," she said, laughing. "He's a friend of my father, and he's got four kids and a wife."

"Well, he looked lonely to me."

She put her arm through mine and pulled herself as close to me as possible.

"This will be a good thing. We can write letters to each other, and I'll let you call me as often as you want."

"Do you mean it?" I tried to joke, and sounding more sarcastic than I had intended.

I would get no pity from her.

"All right, I'll tell you what, it can be your decision. We can either spend the whole evening together celebrating and saying good-bye, after which I could sleep over at Sharon's. Or, I could drive back home right this minute and continue to help my disoriented parents. Who knows, maybe next time you come down I might even have a few free moments to see you. I can't promise anything, seeing how my parents need my constant attention. You decide."

Now, being a member of the Mormon church my whole life, I had been raised to *enjoy* the moment but not to *live* for the moment. After all, our souls are eternal, and if we go jumping toward every instant fulfillment, our eternity could be adversely affected. But at this instant, living for the moment seemed monumentally better than waving good-bye to her and hoping she had a safe trip home. I thought about praying for an answer, but her physical being was a psalm that sang of my decision. She would go to Spain—as if I truly had anything to do with that decision anyway—and tonight we would be together.

24

FLIGHTY

The doors were closed. I could break them open or insist that one of the flight people let me onto the plane to give my pretend sister her medicine. I let the truth run through my head. She was gone. In a second she would be in the air and on her way to Spain. It would be months now until I saw her again, and what then? Would she need to take a short jaunt to the Orient to decide which wedding dress was right for her?

I somehow managed to lose my ticket for the parking garage and was forced to pay the maximum fee.

"How do I know you weren't parked here all night?" the parking lot attendant asked.

"Because you just saw me come through forty-five minutes ago," I pointed out. My reasoning fell on deaf ears.

"Twelve dollars."

I paid him, and he used his power to open the striped arm that had been blocking my progression.

I took three showers that night, hoping to clean out the sick feeling in my gut. Before all three I forgot to hang a dry towel near enough that I could reach it. So, after each shower I had to walk across the cold tile floor dripping like crazy to get a towel.

The third time, I slipped and fell on my wrist, knocking the huge bottle of uncapped shampoo off the rim of the tub. It spilled liberally over the floor. A myriad of swearwords filled my head, petitioning to be let out, but the pattern of my life prevented me from saying anything more than a mildly strong word. Lying on the cold tile floor, drenched in shampoo and thinking about the fourth shower I was going to have to take to rinse off, provided the perfect setting for evaluating my life.

Bronwyn was gone, our engagement temporarily postponed. My mom, dad, brother, and sister, and whoever they happened to be attached to at the moment were living in my house. My house. I had built it. I had raised it from the dust. I was given a piece of charred land, and I had made something out of it more personal than anyone could ever understand. I was sharing this part of me, knowing full well that my family would probably sit on the counters of my heart and nick the walls of my soul. That house was supposed to be Bronwyn's and mine, and now my whole family was shacked up in it and Bronwyn was in Spain.

For my fourth shower I remembered to hang a towel nearby. Self-pity made my senses quite keen.

"So I guess this is good-bye for now," Ed's hand shot out for one last, firm handshake.

"Quite a year," I managed to say.

"Boy, you're telling me. You're still planning to be my best man, aren't you?"

"Wouldn't miss it for the world, Ed."

Ed picked at something on his velour shirt, without speaking, apparently unwilling to trust his voice in the emotion of the moment.

"You all right?" I asked.

He nodded, then swallowed hard. "Fine, fine, I've just had such a good year. You know, you may not believe this, but there was a time that I thought I wouldn't marry. You know, just not the right girl out there. But then you helped fate bring Sharon and me together. What can I say? I owe you, buddy. People that have gotten our announcements have told my mom that they can't believe how pretty Sharon is."

"She's very pleasant to look at," I said, smiling.

"Well, my friend, I'll see you at my wedding." He pulled me into a hard embrace that I thought was a little excessive.

As Ed drove away I couldn't help thinking back to the first day I had met him. He had gone from corduroy shorts to velour shirts, and from smearing skin cream on his head to accepting his baldness. And even though I still couldn't completely tolerate him for more than a few minutes at a time, he didn't wear on me like he used to.

I took a long walk around the campus. With the semester ended, only a few people were hanging out in the places I now knew so well. Tomorrow I would be home—if such a place actually existed without Bronwyn. My father would appear in court this week for some preliminary hearings. I looked forward to the day when all of this would be cleared up.

I had gotten a letter every day that week from Bronwyn. The unhappiness she expressed over being away from me made me extremely smug.

I sat in our booth at the cafeteria and ate some macaroni salad. I watched a small man cleaning the floor, meticulously moving the mop so as not to miss a single spot. I could only eat macaroni salad as long as I didn't have to look at it, and he was the perfect distraction. He distracted my eyes enough that I did not see the eggs in the salad, but he couldn't distract my soul long enough to forget about Bronwyn. So I left a large portion of my food uneaten in a cafeteria that I would never sit in again.

Our apartment manager gave me back most of my cleaning deposit. I had put down one hundred and fifty dollars, but I only got ninety-five back. Apparently, they had had to call a plumber to unclog the shower drain. I'm sure it was filled with Ed's hair. I had decided to go to school in my hometown next semester. Hopefully Bronwyn and I would be married and living in my home by then. I spent the last night in the apartment completely alone, feeling a little sorry for myself.

The beds were the only furniture still in our apartment, so I lay on mine and thought about Joseph Smith in Liberty Jail. My plight was nowhere near his: He had ceilings so low he couldn't stand; I had a home overrun with ungrateful family. He was without his dear friend and brother Hyrum; I was slightly missing Ed's color TV that he had taken with him. Joseph had Emma and her undying love and devotion for him; I had only the latest letter from Bronwyn with a picture of her and a grinning tour guide named Julio, standing in front of the Madrid Temple.

"And if thou shouldst be cast into the pit, or into the hands of murderers, and the sentence of death passed upon thee; if thou be cast into the deep; if the billowing surge conspire against thee; if fierce winds become thine enemy; if the heavens gather blackness, and all the elements combine to hedge up the way; and above all, if the very jaws of hell shall gape open the mouth wide after thee, know thou, my son, that all these things shall give thee experience, and shall be for thy good."

That was the comfort Joseph was given.

Me? Though I prayed and prayed for hours, all I got was an overwhelming urge to eat the few things still left in the refrigerator.

25

LOCKED TIGHT

It was a beautiful ceremony, Ed."

"Thanks," he gushed. "I can't wait to go to yours."

"I can't either."

"Have you two set a date yet?" Ed asked, waving across the room to Sharon, who sat surrounded by her sisters and an assortment of women. The turnout for their reception was astounding. They all must have been friends of Sharon.

"No date yet," I disclaimed. "Bronwyn wants everything to be cleared up. So who knows, it could be years from now before we actually pull it off."

"That's great, Ian," Ed ignored me. "I'd better get back to Sharon."

I figured I had reached an all-time low. Even Ed didn't care. I ate a couple of cookies, laughed to myself about the fact that Ed and Sharon had decorated the cultural hall with helium-filled balloons, and then sneaked out.

The reception was a couple of hours away from home, but the drive went quickly. Soon I was turning onto my road. The summer had peaked and was now steadily running downhill into fall. In a few days Bronwyn would be back, but it still seemed so far away. My brother had helped me pave my driveway—I almost missed the ruts and bumps that used to trumpet my arrival. This eight acres meant everything to me. It was the rock that we were all now clinging to.

Clay and Brittany were finally engaged. Meanwhile, Kate and Mike had set another tentative date to marry. So even with all the legal problems, my parents could see a light of hope somewhere in the distant future. Once my mother even said that if my father didn't wrongly end up in jail and if all her children did have a home, she would like to go on a mission. But not to someplace hard; she wanted to go on one where she could just stand in a temple visitor's center and greet people.

I tried to smile and act happy. After all, life for everyone was moving along. It was only myself that I needed to work on. Unfortunately, the cure for my ailment was still thousands of miles away. I suppose I just wanted something to happen. Anything, for that matter. My life seemed to lack the least bit of adventure or excitement at the moment. It seemed as if things were happening for others, but I was just standing by. I couldn't wait for Bronwyn to return and spice things up. I was sick of renting movies and reading books in hopes of making my time seem important and fulfillling. I was ready for the real thing.

Two more days and counting.

26

THE RECONNECTION

I could never express or convey the emptiness and uncertainty I felt buried in while Bronwyn was away. Her letters made certain moments bearable but did little to chip away at the giant tumor-like void that her absence caused. I worried constantly about her, remembering what I had always known: that she and I were meant to be together. The summer had been one long trip to the dentist—painful and extremely uncomfortable. Now, however, it looked like the fillings were complete and the root canal averted. She was coming home today.

My desire for everything to be perfect when she arrived turned me into a huge mess of tension and impatience. The situation didn't improve when I found that Kate had borrowed the shirt I was planning to wear to the airport and hadn't bothered to tell me.

"Well, where is it now?" I complained.

"Calm down, I don't know. It's either in the dirty clothes hamper or Mike's backpack."

"Kate, you didn't ask to borrow my shirt, and if you had, I probably would have said no. So why did you?"

"Why did I what?" she asked.

"Why did you borrow my shirt without asking?" I moaned.

"Why should I ask when I know you're going to say no? Besides, it wasn't me that wanted to borrow it, it was my friend Jenny. She needed to wear it to match her boyfriend who has one just like it. They got two dollars off the admission price to the amusement park because they were wearing matching shirts." Kate smiled as if she had defeated me with that answer. I threw my arms up and walked away without saying what I was thinking.

I ended up wearing a plain white T-shirt, a sign of surrender. I don't know why, but my faith in mine and Bronwyn's relationship was wavering. We had been apart too long. She had said she needed to find herself. Did that mean when she decided to say yes to marriage that she was lost?

As I was walking through the kitchen, Mom pulled me into the garage so that we could talk privately.

"Do you think the engagement will still be on?" she asked me.

"I think everything's still on," I said, irritated that she would ask such a question.

"I'm just a little concerned, what with the thing she's been through before and all."

Mom pulled a string off my shirt and rolled it between her fingers. She still referred to Bronwyn's previous marriage as a "thing." Occasionally she would call it a messy situation, but for the most part it was just a "thing."

"Don't worry, Mom. To the best of my knowledge,

Bronwyn still likes me. Whether or not we get married on the exact date we planned is the only thing I'm unsure of," I lied.

"You mean you'll get married later or something?"

"Later or sooner. Who knows?" The things I was saying were appeasing my mom, but doing nothing to comfort me.

"I just don't see how you can hope to have a secure and happy marriage with that thing always hanging over your head. And why did she just take off and go to Spain when things got tough? Sounds unstable to me, unstable and insecure. You know how I felt about your father retiring early. He was a big chicken. He ran away, and look what happened because of it; we lost everything and had to move in with our son. Bronwyn's family has always thought that they were better than us, and now she wants to step back and see if my son is good enough for her to marry."

The truth had reared its ugly head. This whole thing was a competition of sorts, and Mom was cracking under the pressure of it.

"Mom, would you do me a tremendous favor and leave Bronwyn and me out of your competition?"

My mom was flustered by my tone of voice.

"Are you putting on weight?" she asked.

It was her last resort, and I just let it roll off my back. Especially because I hadn't put on any weight. In fact, I was in better shape than I had ever been. For the first time in my life, vanity and I were flirting with each other.

"I've got to go, Mom." I kissed her on the forehead and left.

Bronwyn's flight wouldn't arrive for a few hours, so I drove slowly and thought. At one point Bronwyn had said yes. She had committed herself to marrying me then; why should it be any different now? I would pick her up, we would realize that we still wanted the same thing, and that would be that.

I drove around some of the nicer neighborhoods looking at houses that were, in my opinion, too big for human habitation. A big pink house with white garage doors winked at me as cars pulled in and out of it.

I thought that her going to Spain was a pretty good idea. I mean things were pretty mixed-up. And the time away sounded like a temporary solution and a positive step toward making sure that what we did was well thought-out and meant to be. I wanted to do the right thing just as much as she did. But I also didn't want anyone or anything to make what was right look wrong. After all, marriage was a good thing, and we were of age.

I watched a cop pull a white sports car over. The driver of the white car beat his head against the steering wheel as the cop casually walked up to his window.

What if she was now in love with a Spaniard? Some Julio, with incredibly dark hair and brown skin that made him look healthier than he really was? Her last letter was positive, but maybe she was just waiting to break it to me in person. It would be just like her to be concerned about me and my feelings as she was falling in love with another guy.

I looked at my feet on the pedals of my dad's car. I had serious reservations about the shoes I had chosen to wear. Who was I kidding? I had known the moment that Bronwyn had said yes that something had to be wrong. She was way out of my league, and I had been a fool to ever think differently. She had stepped away from the situation, and not too long from now would be giving me the bad news.

I parked and read her last letter for the one hundredth time. I went through the motion of wiping my eyes, even though there were no tears there. I looked out the car window and sighed. I started the car and drove five miles over the speed limit in hopes of breaking the depression. It didn't work; all it did was get me to the airport a few minutes earlier than I had wanted. I parked in front of pillar Q, level number 3. Some family—all of them wearing clogs—almost trampled me as I walked in the airport door. I was incredibly nervous. I felt like I had just gotten off an all-day ride on a roller coaster, and now I was expected to walk and act normally. I checked the arrival screen.

On time.

I went to the gift shop and bought some more mints. I thought about buying some flowers to give Bronwyn as she got off, but I knew that the odds of her bringing some Spaniard home with her would increase if I was standing there holding flowers. So it wasn't as if I didn't think she deserved them; I was just decreasing my odds of a letdown.

I went straight to the rest room to see if I looked as pale as I felt. Nope. Outwardly I was faking it pretty well. While looking in the mirror, I bumped into Marty, a guy from the singles ward. His mother was coming in on the same flight as Bronwyn.

"Wow," he said. "What a coincidence. Want to wait for the flight together?" he asked.

"Sure, I guess." No, I knew.

"Great," Marty hollered.

"I'll wait for you outside," I quickly walked out and took

off in the opposite direction. I could think of nothing worse than waiting for Bronwyn with Marty hanging around. What was he doing at the airport an hour early to pick up his mom? I could feel a headache coming on, so I slowed my pace. What if she wasn't attracted to me anymore? What if she did want to call it off? What hope did I have of finding someone I could be happy with when I would have to use her as a measuring stick? I had written her almost every day. Was that too much? Had I overdone it? Had I made myself so available that she now wanted someone more challenging? I couldn't stand it any longer. Like me or not, I couldn't wait to see her. And even though the odds of her and I ever kissing again seemed less than that of my winning the state lottery, the mere thought of it made the hairs on my neck stand up and turned my heart into a puddle of runny ketchup. I stopped and leaned against a big pillar. I was so nervous that I couldn't catch my breath and walk at the same time. I moved to the arrival screen to see if she was still coming in on time.

Arriving early.

I fell down onto a nearby bench. She was coming five minutes early. Would I be prepared? I should have got my hair cut. It was short already, but I still should have gotten it cleaned up. And the white T-shirt; I should have dug though Mike's backpack and washed the shirt I had intended to wear. With each second that passed, I convinced myself more and more that Bronwyn was a cold, untouchable monument, which I would never be allowed to possess. Not now, not after the distance and the time apart. She had awakened to the situation, while I had dozed off and let her get away.

I slowly walked back to the gate. I was now willing to

throw myself into the clutches of Marty and his nonstop mouth. Who knows, maybe I would hit it off with Marty's single mom? I went back into the rest room and splashed water on my face. It had been some time since I had left the rest room, yet Marty was just coming out of the stall.

"I thought you were going to wait outside," he said. I couldn't believe it; my life was over. We walked out into the concourse together.

"I don't know if you've heard," Marty said, "but the bishop really thinks my plan . . ."

I tuned him out; the nervousness in my gut was too great. It took all I had just to continue standing. She was coming home. She would be here in a matter of minutes. Her hair, her face, her feet, all of her home at last, or at least.

Outwardly I think I looked all right, calm that is. But my insides had taken just about enough. Time was moving too quickly, and I couldn't seem to sit still very much longer. Marty had taken maybe two breaths since we had left the rest room. In between those breaths he had gone on and on about his mother and all the fun she had had while on vacation. I had gotten up a few times to walk off my nervousness, and he had always followed. I finally told him to stop following me and leave me alone. I hurt him, but it worked.

I paced in front of the snack bar, then walked twice around the atrium. No luck—I was just getting more nervous. I didn't know if I could continue to walk or even stand up. I kept eyeing all the airport wheelchairs I passed. I leaned against one of the trash receptacles and tried to regain my composure. Then some insensitive person announced over the intercom that flight 546 had arrived. That did it. My eyes became itchy, my knees went weak, and my gut started turning in ways it had never turned before. I forced my feet to move me to a position where I could watch her come off and greet her without being in the way of anyone else.

They announced the unloading of her flight. I wanted a brown paper bag to breathe into and prevent myself from hyperventilating. The doors flew open, and people began flowing through them. I needed to sit down and put my head between my legs to get some blood to my brain. But I had to appear strong, like this was no big deal.

I was strong.

I had to sit down; this was a big deal. I fought off the urge and remained standing.

Marty's mom came out of the doors. She and Marty greeted each other like two Publisher's Clearinghouse sweepstakes winners. My nervousness was winning—I had to sit down.

I sat.

I saw the top of some hair and jumped back up. It was her. I could hardly breathe. I untucked my shirt, not having the slightest idea what else to do. I was hidden enough that she couldn't see me right off. I watched her marvelously blue eyes look around as she continued to get closer. I stepped through the people in front of me, as if this were a western and I was now showing myself to the foe.

She saw me.

Now I couldn't breathe at all.

She was alone and smiling at me.

I was so light-headed that my legs holding out became a major concern. I was going to throw up. I smiled back and acted as calm as I could.

She started running toward me.

I didn't know what to do. I turned as if to run away, but it was too late. She threw her arms around me and buried her beautiful face in the crook of my neck. I hugged her back, the nervousness in me turning to a realization of how much I had missed her. I pulled her face back enough so that I could look into her eyes. She was crying. The tears ran down her cheeks and past her mouth that was smiling and saying things like, "I love you." "I missed you." "I can't believe I'm home." My chest felt like wet putty.

She was home.

My eyes gave out and tears flowed as I pulled her closer. Light surrounded us like a giant halo, and heaven hummed its approval. Actually, it was just the noise from one of those little airport passenger carts. This, however, was no time to nitpick.

Bronwyn was home.

27

STEPPING IN IT

It was still light as Bronwyn and I sat parked at the edge of Thomas Kane Community Park. The park resided across the street from the Brasswood Building, and from where we were we could see through the front doors and into the lobby. We had pulled over and parked there because it seemed somehow fitting. The building was empty and stood there as a giant reminder of some of the things we now needed to address. Neither one of us wanted to talk; the things we needed to say would likely threaten the happiness we now felt.

The park began to empty out as big black clouds and distant rumbling thunder chased everyone away. Our relationship seemed to invite rain. I decided to be a man and let her start the conversation.

"Forever is a long time," she said.

I wasn't sure what she meant by that so I remained silent.

"I mean, you could get sick of me."

"Never," I insisted.

For some reason my nose began to run, so I reached into

the glove compartment and pulled out a Kleenex. Nothing ruins a mood like blowing your nose. Bronwyn looked at me and tried not to laugh. She was able to stop her mouth, but she couldn't control the humor in her eyes.

We both sighed.

A burst of wind wailed loudly and shook the car.

I looked over at her.

"I love you, Bronwyn." I couldn't help but say it. Sure, other things in life were important, but she was beautiful, and home. It was her fault she got me hooked on her. From the first time I saw her, her every move had driven me crazy. Like some sort of wonderful drug, she sat in my medicine cabinet taunting me, knowing that I could never get past her childproof lid. But I had. I had matched up the arrows and popped open her tightly sealed cap, and now I was pulling out the cotton in hopes of reaching the eternal cure.

My pronouncement of love got very little attention.

"Look," she said, pointing toward the building.

A car just like her father's had pulled into the parking lot.

"Isn't that your father's car?"

She nodded.

Trevor Innaway got out of the car, and then out of the passenger side my dad emerged.

"What are they doing together?" Bronwyn said.

Trevor said something to my dad; then they got back in the car and drove away.

"Our fathers don't hang out with each other," I whispered, as if they might actually hear us from so far away. "Why would they come here together? You don't think they're planning to blow the place up or anything, do you?"

I could sense Bronwyn was just about to tell me not to be

stupid, when from around the east corner of the building our fathers appeared again, this time on foot. My dad unlocked the door as Trevor looked around, and then they both slipped inside. We could see my father through the gray glass, relocking the door, and then they were gone.

"They're going to get caught," Bronwyn moaned.

"Who's going to?" I asked.

"Our dads," she said, raising her voice. "Someone's going to catch our dads opening up the safe or something."

That neither of us was completely convinced that our fathers were innocent was beginning to show.

"Opening the safe?" I wanted to laugh. "This isn't the Wild West or some old-fashioned bank robbery. Nobody's going to find some safe hanging open and start shooting. This is the age of computers and secret combinations; it's much more complicated than that."

"Well, how am I supposed to know that? My dad never taught me about breaking in and secret combinations stuff."

We were raising our voices with each other—not a good thing. I looked at my watch so that I could write down in my journal the exact time it happened.

I stared at the Brasswood Building, twenty-one stories of glass, steel, and cement. I remembered how when I was much younger my dad and I would stand about where Bronwyn and I were now parked, and he would ask, "Do you know which floor your dad's office is on, my boy?"

I always knew the answer, but I would let him tell me.

"The very top floor," he would say, stretching out his arm until his finger pointed directly at the highest floor.

He would then say in almost a whisper, "Do you know why it's on the top floor?"

"No," I would play along.

"Because I'm on top of things," he would then laugh hard and squeeze my shoulder.

Now that same building, the building that I had spent many hours in, cleaning sinks, sat there, black and hard. It was getting dark and cold. Steam was gathering on the inside of the car windows because of our breathing.

"Finally," I said without thinking.

"Finally what?" Bronwyn asked.

"Finally I'm steaming up the car windows with a girl," I said lamely.

Her neck was exquisite looking as she chastised me, and I would have told her so, but another person approached the door of the building, giving me cause to pause. It was Fred Oaks, the biggest fish in the building. He rubbed the top of his head in an attempt to scratch his right eye. He then unlocked the door and slipped in, apparently without bothering to relock it.

"You know, we could go in," I suggested.

"What good would that do?" she asked, her voice indicating that she actually liked the idea.

So, as if I knew what I was doing, I pulled the keys out of the ignition and opened my door.

"I'm coming with you," Bronwyn insisted.

I decided right then was a good time to let know Bronwyn what an open-minded guy I was when it came to women doing whatever they wanted.

We jumped out of the car, and I grabbed her hand. We ran to the building, pulled open the door, leaped in, and in the darkness dove behind a huge potted plant. The only light in the foyer came from the green exit signs over the front doors.

It occurred to us how silly it was, sneaking around like that, and we started to laugh.

"Shhh, they'll hear us," I whispered.

That made us laugh even harder.

The position we were in made it impossible for me to look anywhere but into Bronwyn's left ear. She had, I decided, a most glorious left ear.

It was raining now, the dark sky being illuminated by frequent bolts of lightning. I sat up and then quickly lay back down when I spotted someone else outside the door. The someone pushed into the building and pulled the door shut behind him. As he paused to lock the door, lightning flashed. It was Brian Shakespeare.

I glanced at Bronwyn. Her ear wiggled as she adjusted her mouth to a size bigger than gaping. I put my hands over her mouth to prevent her from screaming and pulled her back down. Brian didn't hear or see us as he hurried toward the elevators. I removed my hands from Bronwyn's mouth.

"What is he doing here?" Bronwyn whispered.

"I have no idea," I answered. "Maybe we should just get out—"

"No way," she hissed. "I want to know what is going on. What are our fathers doing here, in the building they swore that they would never enter again? And why is Brian here? Maybe we can catch him doing something wrong and get him locked up."

The thought of Brian behind bars made me happy.

We decided that taking the elevators was too risky and agreed to take the stairs. We tried to sneak, but our wet shoes squeaked against the marble floor as we made our way to the stairwell door. I couldn't decide how to feel. One part of me wanted to think that we were playing some sort of innocent game in a building in which I clearly had an advantage. I knew every nook and cranny that existed in here. The other part of me was worried. I knew there was something wrong with this particular assortment of people being in the building after-hours, maybe something sinister. I also knew that there was a lot of money involved in the losses the company had suffered—enough money to make the stakes desperately high. I reached to push open the door to the stairwell.

"Wait!" Bronwyn whispered, pulling me back into the alcove.

We could hear footsteps. Someone came running through the darkened foyer toward the elevators. We held our breath, hoping we wouldn't be seen. The someone turned out to be Fred Oaks, he of the tiny head and spread-out features. He punched the elevator button.

"Come on . . ." he complained.

The elevator arrived and dinged. Fred looked over at us with the top of his head and stepped in. The elevator doors closed with him in it.

"I think he saw us," I whispered.

"No, he didn't," Bronwyn said, pushing me through the door marked "Stairs" into the dimly lit stairwell.

"You don't understand," I explained. "That wasn't a comb-over, it was his raised eyebrows."

The elevator dinged again. He was coming back. I pulled Bronwyn into the shadow beneath the stairs, wrapping my arms around her and resting my chin against the back of her head. She failed to see the romance of the situation. The stairway door opened and Fred walked in. We could see and hear him clearly. Well, aside from the fact that his face looked constantly out of focus.

"Ian," he yelled up the stairs. "You kids don't know what you're doing."

We didn't even breathe, afraid of being spotted. What seemed like hours later, but was probably no more than thirty seconds, he swore, turned, and walked out the stairwell door.

"What are we going to do?" Bronwyn whispered.

"What did he mean by 'kids'?" I answered.

Before Bronwyn could tell me to grow up, a door many floors above us in the stairwell opened and closed. We listened as someone descended. Whoever it was seemed to be taking the steps eight at a time, and as he got closer we could hear him grunting. His feet banged loudly above our heads as he passed right over us, and with a swift jolt, he was out the door.

"I think that was my dad," Bronwyn said excitedly, taking off after him.

"Are you sure?" I questioned. "It looked like Brian to me."

I was up and right behind her. We stepped out the door. I grabbed her, and with as much kindness as I could muster at the moment, I told her to shush. We were in the main corridor now and every time she called out, her voice bounced off the glossy marble walls. I was about to explain to Bronwyn the importance of being quiet and how I didn't think it was her dad when suddenly, a few feet in front of us was Brian Shakespeare. That shut her up.

"Well, look who's here," he said. His voice was shaky, and

I could tell he was not exactly pleased to see us. "My little ex-wife and sink boy, Ian. Did you come to take another cheap swing at me?" Lightning flashed. He was standing next to the wall, and his face reflected off the simulated marble that I myself had wiped thousands of fingerprints off of. A following clap of thunder made us all jump.

"Listen——" I tried.

"No," he interrupted. "Now, why don't you tell me what you're doing here?"

Bronwyn opened her mouth as if to tell him exactly what she thought of him. I started talking before she got a chance to make things worse.

"We're here by mistake," I said, squeezing Bronwyn's hand. "We were just trying to get out."

"Oh, so you would like to be let out into the rain?" His voice was flat and lifeless.

"Yeah," I said. "We met in the rain."

I don't know why I said that, it was a complete lie—and not even the kind of lie that makes you look good; it was the kind that leaves you feeling like an idiot.

"I mean, we like the rain." What was wrong with me? I had successfully made a stupid remark even stupider.

Bronwyn shook her head in embarrassment.

"Well, I'll be glad to let you out," he said, moving even closer to us.

It could have been inspiration, or perhaps the uncomfortable feeling of someone invading our personal space. Either way, Bronwyn and I both simultaneously began backing away from him.

"What's the matter?" Brian said to Bronwyn in an oily voice. "Don't you trust me?"

227

"It makes me sick just to look at you," she said boldly.

"That's not what you used to say." He smiled icily.

He then stepped quickly toward us. That was our cue to run; we turned and bolted. With no time to wait for the elevator, we ran to the stairs, threw open the door, jumped inside, and leaned against the door to keep it closed. Brian began to bang on it with his hands. After a moment the banging stopped, and we thought we heard footsteps walking away. We looked at each other. There was no place to go but up.

The second floor door was locked. So was the third, fourth, fifth, and so on. By the time we reached the twenty-first floor I wanted to fall down and complain about how tired I was, but Bronwyn didn't even seem out of breath. Pride kept me from displaying my weariness and made me act as if the multilevel climb was nothing out of the ordinary for me. The door into the hallway was unlocked. I didn't know whether we should feel lucky or not.

The door opened soundlessly, and we stepped into the dark hallway. It was now pitch black out and raining like the days of Noah. We were on the top deck of our multi-million-dollar ark hoping that the lightning would hurry and show the way before the waters engulfed us. The only light was some seeping out beneath a closed door and the dim glow of the exit sign over the stairwell.

"This is ridiculous," Bronwyn whispered. "I just returned home from Spain to the guy I love, and the first night back we spend locked in a dark building being chased by my ex-husband while looking for our fathers."

I kissed her, bothered that she would bring up her

ex-husband while we were together. Lightning and thunder struck simultaneously.

I grabbed her hand and pulled her down the hall toward the one lit room. I pushed the door open and the room looked empty. We stepped inside. A number of the large filing cabinet drawers were open and papers were scattered everywhere. The thunder and lightning were coming non-stop now, and the rain was blowing hard against the building. Suddenly, the sky exploded and all the lights went out.

"Perfect," Bronwyn said, trying to sound okay with all of this.

We felt our way back down the hall. Thunder struck and Bronwyn screamed and fell to the floor, holding her leg.

"What happened?" I yelled.

"My leg," was all she said.

I knelt down and could feel . . . blood coming from her leg. I couldn't believe it; she had been shot. A bullet had hit her in the calf.

"I think you've been shot," I said in disbelief.

She leaned her head against me and then did what I was on the verge of doing myself. She passed out.

I looked up to see two dark forms standing over us. Thanks to my father's full figure I could tell it was him, and Brother Innaway. I suddenly felt awful about how poorly I was taking care of his daughter.

"Ian?" my dad asked in amazement. "What are you two doing—"

"Someone shot her," I blurted.

Brother Innaway got down on his knees beside his daughter.

"Who did this? Did you see anyone?" I couldn't clearly

see his face, but his voice was stressed enough to let me know that he was not happy.

"I don't know who did it. We were trying to get out of the building, and I thought it was thunder, but someone has shot her."

"I can't believe you two are here. You're supposed to be at the airport." My dad didn't sound happy either.

I took off my jacket, ripped it apart, and tied it around Bronwyn's leg. Even amidst the confusion and fear I felt very Boy Scoutish.

"We've got to get her out of here," I said, taking control of the situation. "We can talk about all this other stuff later, but we have got to get her some help."

"We were only trying to clear our names, Ian," my dad said, acting as if he owed me an explanation. "Brian is the one who has caused all this trouble, and Fred has the proof."

"Why didn't you just tell the cops?"

"We needed to know for sure."

"It was a stupid idea," Brother Innaway lamented. "But we could see no other way."

"Let's just get her out of here," I said, grabbing Bronwyn under her arms. Her father took her legs, and as quickly as we could, we shuffled across the hallway and to the elevators. They didn't work. We moved to the stairwell. Emergency lights gave the stairs a small amount of light.

About six flights down, Bronwyn began to stir.

"It's going to be all right," I said. "Just a few minutes more and we'll be out of here. Do you think you can make it?"

"Some welcome home," she smiled wearily.

I wanted to wish this away; I wanted us to be back out in

the car, holding hands and just viewing the problem from a distance. Distracted by my wandering mind, I lost my footing and Bronwyn slipped from my grasp. She didn't hit hard, but I don't think my accident did anything to improve my relationship with her father.

"I'm so sorry," I said to her.

Again she smiled—or maybe it was a wince.

After a few rests we made it to the bottom, only to find the door leading out of the stairs was now locked from the outside.

Bronwyn's dad swore.

We laid Bronwyn down. I was thoroughly winded, and wind and thunder continued to howl and explode, making our minds and the situation that much more unsettled.

I was going to suggest that we say a prayer, but Trevor Innaway swore again.

"Dad, we'll be all right," Bronwyn said weakly.

"When we went up before," I told them, "the only door we could get through was the top floor. I'll climb back up and then come down the utility shaft that runs alongside the elevator and see if I can open this door from the other side."

Our dads both nodded.

I looked at Bronwyn, smiled, and started climbing stairs before I could chicken out. By the time I made it to the top floor my lungs were really shot. My spirit was equally wounded when I discovered the top door was now locked. Someone had gone out of their way to lock us in. With no other option I went down a few floors and found a vent big enough to crawl through. I kicked it open, crawled through it, and then lowered myself through the ceiling of the eighteenth floor.

I tried flicking switches in hopes of getting a little light, but it was useless. Thankfully, my eyes adjusted, and I could see well enough to get around. I moved out of the room I was in and into the hall. The rest rooms on each floor were located right next to the elevator, and at the back of each rest room there was a closet door that opened up into the elevator utility shaft that ran down the length of the building. The doors opening to the shaft were usually locked, but if you turned the handle and kicked hard enough, they would pop open. The trick worked. The shaft was dark but partially lit by the small emergency lights.

Somewhere, something dripped.

I climbed carefully down the iron ladder, not wanting to slip and fall to my death. Poorly painted numbers indicating each floor kept reminding me how much farther I had to go.

This was all wrong. This night should have gone a lot differently. I should have been looking into the eyes of a non-wounded Bronwyn. We should have been saying stupid things. The kind of things that people in love say and then later pretend that they didn't. This was my train of thought as I reached the tenth floor. I had intended to just keep on going, but a small light shining at the end of one of the ducts caught my eye. It was dim and coming through a room about thirty feet over.

"Just climb down and get out," I kept telling myself, but my body was not responding correctly to my fears. For some reason, I was moving into the duct and crawling toward the light. I reached the glow and peered down through the vent.

A laptop computer was on, and I could see the back of Brian's head directly below me. He was typing frantically. I held my breath and tried not to move.

A door opened and Brian turned. It was Fred. I thought for a moment that all would be well. Fred would bust Brian, and we could all call it a night. Instead, Fred shut the door behind him and Brian nodded.

"I turned the elevator back on," Fred informed him.

"And?" Brian asked, his eyes never leaving the computer screen.

"And they're locked up tightly in the stairwell."

"This is going to work perfectly," Brian said, standing up. "This just needs a few more minutes to copy the files. Pop the disk and bring it with you when it's done. I need to go say a few things to my dear ex-wife and her pathetic friend."

That was me.

"I still owe that clown for sucker-punching me," Brian added.

"Hit him once for me," Fred said, as if wishing me well. "I never liked the funny way he stared at me when he worked here. But use your brain. You can't just go around shooting people, even if she is your ex-wife." Brian left the room, and Fred sat down right below me.

I had no idea what I should do. Brian was heading off to hassle Bronwyn, but Fred was making copies of something that could prove my father's innocence. Fate helped me out. My right arm had fallen asleep and while shifting my weight to relieve it, I broke through the ceiling tile and fell into the room. I landed right on top of Fred. He broke my fall quite nicely. His wide face slammed against the desk, and we rolled down onto the carpet together. I would have tried to apologize, but he was out cold. I took an extension cord that was connecting a printer and two lamps and tied him tightly to a chair.

The laptop chirped as it finished. The timing couldn't have been better. I popped the disk out and put it in my pocket. I would have just left, but I felt I owed Fred a little something extra for asking Brian to hit me once for him. I took a black marker lying on the desk and drew a nice goatee on his face. After dabbling in the arts, I went out into the hall and back into the rest room. My shoulder was really hurting from the fall, but I figured it did no good to whine about it where Bronwyn couldn't hear. Again, turning the knob and kicking the door worked. I was back in the shaft and descending. The dripping noise I had heard earlier was a lubricant that was spilling from a pipe onto the ladder I was now climbing down. My feet kept slipping off the rungs and my hands were barely getting enough grip to hang on. I was so relieved to finally reach the ground floor. My relief was short lived, however. Before I had taken two steps in the direction of the stairs, Brian oozed out in front of me waving a gun.

"So we meet again," Brian said, trying to be dramatic. "I can't believe how much I hate you."

"I wonder if it equals the affection I have for you?"

"Shut up and walk." Lightning was flashing so often that the lobby looked permanently lit, and rain and hail beat relentlessly against the glass walls. Brian shoved me over to the main stairs where Bronwyn had been trapped. But the door was open and there was no one there.

"Where are they?" Brian demanded.

"I have no idea," I answered honestly.

I was relieved that Bronwyn and our fathers had gotten out, but I was now pretty concerned about me. Then the most marvelous thing happened. Suddenly, in a wail of sirens, the outside of the building was illuminated by head-lights and flashing emergency lights of what looked to be at least a thousand police cars—the cavalry had arrived. Brian and I both stood with gaping mouths. He looked at me and swore.

"It's not my fault," I explained.

Brian pushed me around the entire floor looking for a way out. It was pointless; we were officially surrounded.

28

LEFT FOR DREAD

I wanted to shout for joy; instead, I was assailed with a multitude of swearwords and dragged by the arm into the elevator. I was glad—it was a nice break from the stairs. I kept thinking that I should just try to wrench the gun away and beat Brian up. The idea had merit for a whole list of reasons.

I said a quick prayer. *Should I jump him?* I silently asked.

No answer came.

I knew the reason that I was not getting an answer was because every time I thought about Bronwyn getting shot in the calf, the prevailing theme to my thoughts was what nice legs she had. Now when I needed divine intervention the most, the pattern of my not-so-distant past stayed the hand of heaven.

The heavens roared with thunder and disapproval.

I thought about a lesson I had been taught years ago, about Joseph Smith and how he always took the initiative. He didn't wait around. In times of crisis, he made a decision and acted upon it.

I made a decision and waited for the right moment to act upon it.

The elevator reached the top floor and dinged. It was now or never. As the doors opened I leaned as if stepping out and then suddenly threw my head back, smacking Brian hard with the back of my head against his nose. Before he was able to react, I turned and landed one really good punch directly into his face. He grabbed me, and we both tumbled out of the elevator and into the top-floor lobby. I knocked his hand and the gun flew backwards, sliding across the hallway floor. Brian hit me hard in the ear, bringing on a ringing noise identical to the sound TV channels make when they finally go off the air for the night. I stumbled back against the wall and moved to avoid another of his punches. He hit the wall hard and started screaming. I kicked his legs out from under him, then straddled his chest and pinned both his arms with my knees. He wailed frantically and tried to lift his legs up to kick the back of my head. It was futile—I had him. Sadly, I didn't know what to do with him. He was trapped, but I had no way of tying him up or making him do what I said. As long as I sat on top of him he was my prisoner, but if I attempted anything else, the tables could quickly turn.

An idea popped into my head. I needed to hit him until he was unconscious. I don't think it was the still small voice, but I had been taught that it is rude to ignore people, or voices for that matter. Sure, the thought of hitting a person who was unable to hit back made me uneasy. But I thought of Nephi beheading Laban. That, of course, had been for a righteous cause, and the Lord had made it perfectly clear that

Nephi needed to do it. I thought of Joseph Smith again and used the initiative bit to justify my decision.

Rationalizing was one thing I excelled at.

Brian screamed and tried as hard as he could to throw me off.

I had to do this. Thunder ripped across the sky as if giving me a soundtrack to punch by. Brian called me a really bad name, making my first blow even easier to give.

Instantly my mother popped into my head and began chastising me as Brian helplessly tried to block my blows.

"You shouldn't hit people."

Pow!

"It's not nice to hit."

Crack!

"How would you like it if someone hit you?"

Wham!

My mom leaning over my shoulder telling me what not to do gave me added strength. The wind howled, and Brian slurred a final swearword seconds before I landed my last blow.

I got off of him carefully, making sure he wasn't just really good at playing the silent game.

I felt around for the gun. I found it and dropped it behind a potted plant. I looked at Brian lying there peacefully and I sort of wished that it had taken a few more hits to turn him off—he still looked too pretty. I bent over and messed up his hair. That helped a little. I stepped back into the hall and pressed the button for the elevator. It didn't light up. I pressed all of the elevator buttons; none of them lit up. I tried the stairwell, but Fred had done too good a job jamming it shut. My only option for getting out was using the utility shaft again.

I was so tired, most of my body was shaking, and the few parts that weren't wanted only to stay still. My fists were raw and my legs were cramping from climbing up and down. I dreaded the thought of having to climb down that greased iron ladder, but my desire to finally end this and see Bronwyn spurred me on.

I weakly pushed at the door into the shaft and it wouldn't open. I was forced to kick it, and my leg cooperated long enough to get the job done. I was back in the shaft. Descending was slow going. I thought about falling and the fact of death following life. My grandpa had died, and I had handled that pretty well. No one in my family really talked about death; the subject seemed to make all of us uncomfortable. My mom had always said that after she died, she wanted liposuction so that she could look lean in her coffin. She said she was too scared to have it done while she was alive but figured that after she had passed away, and with pain not being a factor, it was something she would like to have done. So my perception of death was someone lying in a coffin with the fat sucked out of her thighs. Not a very pretty thought.

As I passed the fifteenth floor I could hear the sound of the elevator whining. It was working again and going down. I prayed that it was someone with a kind finger who had pressed the button. As I descended past the twelfth floor I heard a different kind of whining.

"I thought you would never get here," Brian said nastily as he stood on the platform at the eleventh floor. His voice startled me, and I almost gave up the ghost right then and there. He was pointing a gun at me.

"You should have hit me harder," Brian sneered. "Or hidden the gun better."

"We all make mistakes," I said, trying not to reveal my real fear and noticing that somehow in the last couple of crazy minutes he had found time to comb his hair. His face was still messed up though.

"That's the truth," he laughed. "I should have shot you years ago when you were cleaning out my sink."

"How did you get here?" I asked, amazed that he had beaten me down.

"You just need to learn how to work the elevators."

"This is stupid, Brian," I tried to reason. "You can't shoot me with the whole building surrounded."

Thunder rocked the Brasswood Building as wind howled in protest of being kept out.

"I can do whatever I please," Brian snapped.

"I suppose that explains the way you treated Bronwyn."

He didn't dignify my jab with an answer. He did, however, wave me down and onto the platform with his gun.

"You know," Brian said as I stood directly in front of him, "up until this point I haven't had to kill anyone, but I think you will make a perfect first."

I think I was finally one hundred percent scared. "Come on, this whole thing is stupid, but murder?"

"I'm not going to murder anyone," Brian insisted.

I whewed within.

"I'm simply going to witness your tragic suicide." He gestured to the open utility shaft. "Jump," he commanded.

"Brian." I was begging, and not too proud to do so.

"Jump," he repeated, saying it as if it were just an ordinary word with a minor consequence.

"I know you don't really want to do this."

"I've never wanted anything more. Who knows, maybe when they find you at the bottom, it will be a big enough distraction for me to slip out unnoticed. Now jump!"

His eyes were on fire and his body was obviously in pain. I prayed, a really quick and desperate prayer, but no answer came. I prayed a really quick and honest prayer. I was still there. I prayed a really quick and heartfelt prayer. It was the right combination. From below, someone opened a door to the shaft. It was many floors away, but it was just what God needed to send a fierce wind rushing through the building. It whooshed down the shaft, blowing the door closed right behind Brian. With a pop the door hit him and threw him into me. Twisting, he slid right over the edge into the shaft. I fell on my stomach on the platform and was able to grab his left arm. The tables had turned. I was now holding onto him as he dangled from the ledge.

He swore at me like no one had ever sworn before.

"Grab my other hand," I hollered.

I could see faces many floors down stepping into the shaft and peering up.

Brian directed his eyes toward me, afraid to look down. Then he pointed the gun he was still holding directly at my head.

"If you drop me, I'll kill you," he roared.

"If you kill me, I'll drop you," I countered.

His weight was too great: I didn't have the strength to lift him up, and neither of us had the strength to hold on much longer. His options were spent. He released the gun and let it fall. "Just pull me up," he pleaded.

I shifted and grabbed his other arm. For a brief moment I entertained the thought of just dropping him, but then I pulled the weasel up and onto the platform. He lay limp on his belly, and I put my right foot in the middle of his back to hold him. After a moment police burst in from the rest room.

One of the policemen asked me a few questions and then told me that I needed to come with him. Someone radioed down for the elevator; I was so happy that we wouldn't be taking the stairs. The elevator smelled of sweat and unpleasant body odor. Brian's face looked like stone now—he was showing no emotion—but at about the seventh floor he broke out into an incredibly pitiful sob. I tried really hard to feel sorry for him.

Honest.

I think that literally every cop in the city was there that night. The peaceful parking lot where Bronwyn and I had sat a couple of hours before was now a circus of pouring rain, flashing red and blue lights, and activity. There was even a news helicopter there. My father popped out of a cop car and ran toward me.

The cops questioned me for a while. I gave them the disk I had taken and told them about Fred. They found him right where I had left him. Moments later when they escorted him out of the building I had a hard time not laughing at his marker goatee. I tried to not leave out anything about the night, but I was so beat that I'm not sure exactly what I said to the cops. After Brian ratted on Fred, and Fred squealed on Brian, they were whisked away. My father informed me that while in the stairwell he had remembered that he had keys to open the doors. He apologized for sending me up when it had not been necessary. He seemed genuinely embarrassed. He told me that after they had gotten out they had called the police and the rest was history. He also added that Bronwyn had been taken to the nearest hospital and was in good condition.

I had to see her.

* * * * *

The nurse on duty looked at me like I was a leper, and only after I had given her an extensive overview of the night did she tell me where Bronwyn was.

The door felt heavy as I pushed it open. Bronwyn was sharing the room with someone else—an elderly woman in plaid pajamas who lay snoring in the first bed. I couldn't believe that I was going to see her—Bronwyn that is—and that this night was over. I moved quietly around the curtain dividing the two beds, expecting to find Bronwyn asleep. She was wide-awake and waiting.

"It's about time," she smiled.

I collapsed against her, my legs hanging off the bed and my head resting deep in her hair. She began to cry, not a violent, uncontrollable sob, but a beautiful, tears-of-joy type cry. We exchanged I-love-yous, and glad-it's-overs. I was so tired that I wanted nothing more than to just lie down next to her and sleep, but I was already going to get one heck of a talking to when my mother found out that her son had been hitting people. If I fell asleep with Bronwyn now, no matter how innocent, I would never hear the end of it.

"I only have to stay till tomorrow morning," Bronwyn said. "Do you think you could take me home then?"

I nodded yes.

"So," I asked. "Will you still marry me?"

"I don't know," she said. "You're kind of boring."

I pulled myself up and kissed her, her warm lips making my cold spirit burn.

I would have kept on kissing her, but she pulled back just a bit to whisper, "Yes."

My spirit screamed hallelujah, and my soul danced on the ceiling; but my body collapsed onto a small sofa in the room. Then and there, serenaded by the snoring of a complete stranger and comforted by the presence of the girl I loved, I found sleep.

29

THE DIRT OF KOLOB

All charges were dropped against both our fathers. It took some time to get matters straightened out, but things were so different now—hope saturated everything.

We spent a lot of time in court, recounting and testifying. In the end Brian, Fred, and two other people were convicted of embezzlement and sentenced. I would love to say I understood exactly what they had done, or make the explanation as easy as Mr. Peabody did it in the den with a candlestick. But even after days in court, I only understood a few things. One, the disk I took really helped. Two, Brian was one heck of a criminal. And three, I really liked Bronwyn. The other thing I knew was that our fathers were finally proven innocent.

The relief of having the trial over and the anticipation of the wedding made everyone a little quick to smile and slow to frown. The morning of the wedding I took Ed up to my place in the mountains to get the last of it ready for the wife I was going to be bringing there. Ed talked nonstop as I got ready.

"So, I heard you won't be the only one getting hitched in your family this year," Ed chirped while picking up a small framed picture of Bronwyn and me on the night of our Ferris wheel escapade. "Yep, your mother was telling me that both Kate and Clay are planning to marry as soon as they can. Brittany and Mike will make nice additions to the family."

"I had heard that, too," I said, wondering if Ed remembered that they were my family, not his. "I guess it just takes us Smiths a little time to find the right ones."

"Listen, Ian," he said seriously and not actually listening to me. "I've been thinking about you and Bronwyn living out here in the country, and I've got to say . . . well, it seems like an idea that needs a bit more thinking on." Ed tapped his forehead as if he were hard at thought. "You know, you two could move into the apartment complex Sharon and I are living in down in Sterling. It would be like old times."

I smiled, knowing that those old times were over.

"Thanks, Ed, but I think we'll give it a try out here."

"It's so . . . rural. I'm sure the ward out here is probably a bit unusual. You know these country folks."

"We've gone to the ward, Ed," I said as I zipped up my small suitcase. "It seems quite normal."

"I hope they provide you with the number of service opportunities those wards in town can. Did you know I have two callings at the moment?" Ed beamed.

I beamed back, knowing that one of his callings was making sure that the person who set up overflow chairs put them in straight lines. I checked my watch and decided that it was time to go. There was just one more little thing I wanted to do.

"Ed, do you mind if I have just a moment alone?"

"Be my guest," Ed said, sitting down on the couch.

I decided that I could do the alone thing a whole lot better outside. I walked out onto the porch and closed the door tightly behind me. I looked out over the valley and watched some stark white clouds slowly drifting by.

This was it. In a couple of hours I would be sealed for time and all eternity to Bronwyn. All the birthday candles I had ever blown out and every wishbone I had ever pulled had been accompanied with the wish that she would someday notice me. Now, the fulfillment of that and more was coming to pass. All the lit birthday candles in the world could not have produced the flame of thanks and gratitude that burned within me.

I had gotten the girl.

The autumn sun was warm on my neck as I walked to the far edge of the property.

The north corner was not only the most beautiful part of my land, but it was also the place where I had planted my first two trees. When I saw that one of them was going to survive, I'd decided to dedicate it to my grandfather—it was, after all, his wealth that had made it all possible.

That once-small tree now stood taller than I did.

I could still remember the talk my father and I had had after the first house had burned down. His words, which seemed insensitive and cold then, had been one of the things that motivated me and enabled me to develop the heart and soul of my life.

"I'll be interested to see what you do with it," he had said.

"Well, Dad, here it is," I said aloud, wishing my father could hear me.

This afternoon my "I do's" would be over, and this land would be officially both Bronwyn's and mine. The formalities made little difference; it had all belonged to her many years before. Today, however, she would move from proxy, to present.

I picked up a handful of my soil and then let it fly off with the wind. This burnt field had become a Garden of Eden. True, the snakes acted differently, and I couldn't grow a decent apple, but miracles seemed to surround this plot of land. The dirt of Kolob would be hard pressed to produce the kinds of results this soil had.

I said a short prayer and then walked back to the driveway and put my things into the car. I tried really hard to be sentimental and heavy in regard to the crossroads of life I was now standing on. But it's terribly difficult to be solemn and reflective when the image of what lay ahead is so spectacular. Ed came out of the house and locked the door for me.

"All set?" he asked.

"Ready," I answered honestly.

We hopped into the car and sped into the city as fast as we could.

I had a feeling I was late when I entered the temple foyer and Bronwyn's parents were standing there with their hands on their hips, wearing impatient expressions on their faces. I called them Mom and Dad but it didn't produce the warm bond I had been hoping for. I changed clothes and then was led to the sealing room by a short man with wispy hair and a solid smile. Everything seemed to be moving so rapidly until I saw her.

Bronwyn was spectacular. I hardly noticed anything else.

Sure there were the loved ones and burning feelings and heavenly promises. And yes, the mirrors were there reflecting our image as a forever couple. But more than anything, there was Bronwyn and the realization that *we* were about to become *us*.

Bronwyn took my hand and squeezed in such a manner that I knew I was in for it, in a good way. Amazing words were spoken, and the "I do's" were delivered without complication.

The eternities were shaping up nicely.

ABOUT THE AUTHOR

Robert Farrell Smith lives in Albuquerque, New Mexico, with his wife, Krista, and their daughters Kindred Anne, Phoebe Hope, and Naomi Rose and son, Bennett Williams. Among Robert's works are the novels: *The Miracle of Forgetness; Captain Matrimony; Baptists at Our Barbecue, All Is Swell; Falling for Grace;* and *Love's Labors Tossed.* He is also a contributor to Mormonlife.com and has written over two family newsletters. His writing has been called "farcical," "brilliant," and "ground-breaking." Robert has been called some things also.

If you loved this book, you'll also want to read Robert Farrell Smith's farcical novel *Captain Matrimony*, published by Deseret Book Company.

It's a romance.

It's a mystery.

It's full of surprises . . .

When Andy Phillips gets a job teaching calculus at a high school in his hometown of Charlotte, North Carolina, he thinks he has it made. That is—until the school burns down. That leads him on an unlikely journey to the town of Mishap, Utah, where, besides teaching math, he is called upon to unravel the mystery of a local curse, while trying to win the heart of the girl of his dreams . . .

NOT LONG BEFORE HE DIED, Brigham Young sent a thickheaded farmer named Cornelious Thunder out to the Pinched Basin region in Utah to establish a town.

Cornelious did just that.

He picked a spot between two high red cliffs and at the bottom of the basin. Then when no one was around, he lifted his arms to the heavens and asked God, "Does this have to be the place?" His answer came in the form of two black crows flying headfirst into one another. Cornelious felt this was unusual enough to qualify as a sign. He also was just stubborn enough to make the new town work. He stuck to his guns and with hard work and sheer determination created what became known as Thunder City,

Utah. For many years Thunder City flourished. The red cliffs kept the wind out and the soil together. Trees grew fast and soon what was a shabby piece of desert turned into a spotty green haven people couldn't help but whistle at.

Wearing the blinders of everyday routine, few folks stopped to realize that the entire population of Thunder City was Mormon. This fact became glaringly clear when only a few years back a German immigrant named Reinhold Hap wandered into town looking for a piece of good land to settle on. He had discovered Thunder City one night while surfing the Net in Munich, Germany. The city's home page (yes, it had a home page!) made this piece of Utah look like the perfect all-American town. It also promised low-cost property. Reinhold arrived and bought one of the nicest plots in town, plus a pair of cowboy boots and a matching hat. He built his dream home on his land, which was located near the public library and two blocks over from the city park.

Well, as time rolled on people began to notice and grow curious as to why Reinhold didn't attend church. The bishop actually put sacrament meeting on hold while he sent out the elders quorum to see what was up. When they reached his house Reinhold answered the door and informed them of three things. One and two were that he wasn't a member of their church, and that he would have told them so if only they had asked. Three was that they were interrupting the rerun of *Night Rider* that he was watching. The elders quorum, for the first time in as long as anyone could remember, was silent.

Few knew that there were those in their midst who watched reruns of commercial television on Sunday. Also, it had never occurred to any of them that there would someday be a genuine nonmember living in their town. They were thrilled. Finally they had someone to direct their missionary efforts towards. Reinhold Hap was befriended and prodded by everyone in the area. He was invited to all the Church functions. He was also the guest of honor at Celebrate Reinhold Day. Committees were formed and prayers were offered in pushy earnest, and all on behalf of Reinhold and his unconverted soul. The ward even had a barn raising at his house despite the fact that he already had a barn and didn't need another. In the eyes of Thunder City, Reinhold was an honorary "brother," on his way to becoming the real thing.

Reinhold took it all in stride.

When he said he wasn't interested, folks would just smile and say things about there being a time and a place when he would be. If he argued that he was happy with his own religion, folks would wink and comment about him eventually seeing the light. And when he wanted to start dating some of the older single Latter-day Saint women in town, folks threatened to ride him out on a rusty rail. They further vowed that the day his Gentile hands touched one of their fair women they would stone him, tar him, or drag him down across the border, depending on the mood of the mob. It was one thing to have a nonmember amongst you, but it was an entirely different issue if that nonmember had aspirations of fiddling with your women.

A lesser man might have left Thunder City altogether, but Reinhold Hap liked his piece of earth and felt that he was entitled to stay there and pursue his own happiness. So with a couple of well-written letters he struck up a friendship with a woman he had known back in Munich. Impressed by the way he manipulated ink and attracted to the prospect of a home and two barns, this woman traveled across the world and into the arms of Reinhold Hap. They married in the bigger of the two barns with the help of a preacher from three towns over.

With Reinhold married off, the townsfolk figured they could treat him neighborly again. Reinhold wouldn't have it. He insisted that everyone leave him and his wife alone. He also threatened that if he ever caught a single person calling him "Brother" he wouldn't be able to control himself. So in a town full of Brothers and Sisters, there was only one Mr. and Mrs. Hap.

Shortly into the new marriage, tragedy struck the Haps. On a particularly cloudy morning Harriet Hap turned up missing. The back door of their house was torn off and unknown footprints were spotted in the wet garden soil. Reinhold swore he had no idea what had happened to her or where she could be, but that didn't hide the fact that she was gone.

The town suspected foul play.

Stones were turned and bushes trimmed in an effort to search thoroughly. After two months of nothing, the town put the pins on Reinhold. Surely, he had to know what had happened. Or maybe *he* was the *what*. Everyone knew that things had not been ideal for Reinhold and Harriet. There had been many signs that the marriage was having problems shortly before her disappearance. Those signs now seemed to suggest that something truly bad had happened and that Reinhold was the cause.

There was a short trial that ended in a mistrial and

mistrust. Reinhold withdrew, hiding himself up in his house and coming out only to yell at the kids who were brave enough to cross his lawn to buy milk and cheese at the corner store. He claimed Thunder City had ruined his marriage and his life. He cursed everyone, threatening that his misery would be heaped upon the heads of any townsperson who married. He promised nothing but doom and misfortune to those who chose matrimony.

Larry and Tillie Cutler were the first couple to thumb their noses at Reinhold and his curse. They had married in the Salt Lake Temple and had an elaborate reception in Thunder City. After the reception, the happy couple packed into the small plane Larry owned and flew off for their honeymoon and into what should have been a happy future. And it may well have been just that, if not for the small fact that the two of them were never seen again. Their plane simply disappeared and no part of it had yet been found. Exhaustive searches and studies were made; lakes were dragged and theories tossed about like extra pennies into a watery well. There were those who figured the plane had gone down in some small unknown spot within the thousands of miles that the flight plan covered. But the majority of the town figured Larry and Tillie had simply been taken up in the curse of Reinhold Hap.

Everyone was stunned. Reinhold withdrew even further from the community, locking himself up in his big house and showing his face so seldom that few folks remembered what he looked like. The rest of the town mourned, feeling that somehow they were all to blame. It had never been their intention for things to end this way, but when they really looked at it most people seemed to realize just how much their actions had contributed to the end.

The town was bruised.

People might have gone on and on forever, rehashing and recalling the things they had done to make this happen if it hadn't of been for the reappearance of Mrs. Hap.

Of course it wasn't like Harriet to simply walk back into town one day and ask if anyone had missed her. No, apparently she had more flair than that. She first appeared on a stormy night, the apparition of her face spreading across the choppy water of Knock Pond. The image looked like no more than distorted light until one of the youth climbed up on top of Lop Rock and saw to his horror that the picture before him was that of Harriet Hap. The movement of water seemed to contort her face and give her lips shape.

"Marriage," she seemed to whisper. "Marriage."

After she had spoken her piece she faded back into the dark water. But not from memory. Since that night she had appeared many times, always forming across the surface of the pond like some two-dimensional demon. And always whispering the name of the union that had been the death of her.

The townsfolk of Thunder City had attempted to figure out how she appeared and why, but no reasonable answers had ever come of it. But the town talked and thought of her so often that eventually most folks began calling the place "Mrs. Hap."

"Mrs. Hap" became "Mishap" and the city became forever changed—it simply lost some of its thunder.

FROM CHAPTER FOUR OF *CAPTAIN MATRIMONY*